MU VESS

A Sila

Murder on Orford Ness

A Silas Quirk Mystery, Volume 2

Andrew Hixson

Published by Andrew Hixson, 2026.

This is a work of fiction. Similarities to real people, places, or events are entirely coincidental.

MURDER ON ORFORD NESS

First edition. October 30, 2026.

ISBN: 979-8233880230

Written by Andrew Hixson.

Also by Andrew Hixson

A Silas Quirk Mystery
Murder on Mersea Island
Murder on Orford Ness

To Julie, Michelle, Louise, Ava, Summer, Sienna, and Sapphire.

About the Author

Andrew Hixson was born in Barnet and is married with two daughters, three granddaughters, and two cherished granddogs. Now living in Suffolk, Andrew preserves a strong loyalty to Arsenal Football Club, following their fortunes from afar. He enjoys reading, attending both cinema and theatre, and playing golf whenever his back permits.

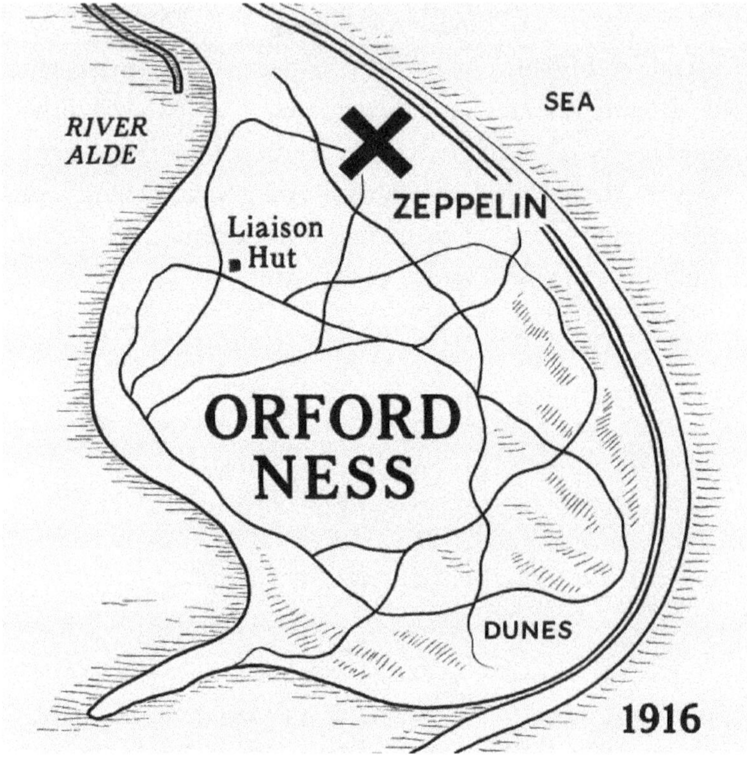
SEA
RIVER ALDE
ZEPPELIN
Liaison Hut
ORFORD NESS
DUNES
1916

MURDER ON ORFORD NESS

WAR HIDES MANY CRIMES. This one was meant to vanish in fire.

In 1916, as German airships prowl Britain's coastline, a Zeppelin crashes on Orford Ness. The War Office calls in Lieutenant Silas Quirk to assess the damage—quietly.

But amid the wreckage, Quirk finds a body that doesn't belong.

The young woman was killed before the crash. And someone used the destruction to erase her murder.

Quirk's investigation draws him into a web of coastal espionage, coded signals, and villagers bound by fear rather than loyalty. As he follows the trail through marshland, lighthouse beams, and whispered confessions, he uncovers a secret network willing to sacrifice anything—including innocence—to survive the war.

Murder on Orford Ness is a richly atmospheric historical thriller and the second instalment in the **Silas Quirk Mysteries**, blending classic detective fiction with wartime espionage and psychological depth.

1

I was not given orders so much as a vacancy where they ought to have been.

There was no paper trail, no file tied with ribbon and impressed with authority. Only a room in Whitehall that smelled of old smoke and damp wool, and a man in uniform who did not give his name. He whispered, as though the walls themselves were inclined to listen.

"A German airship came down on the Suffolk coast," he said. "Two nights ago."

I waited. Silence, in my experience, was often more forthcoming than speech.

"Orford Ness," he added at last. "You are to attend. Observe. Report only to me."

"And what precisely am I to observe?"

His mouth twitched, not quite a smile. "Whatever they didn't intend to be seen."

That was all. By the following morning, London had loosed its hold on me, releasing me eastward as the city thinned into soot-stained outskirts, then into bare fields and a sky drawn low and colourless. The train rattled like an exhausted animal. The windows filmed with breath and steam. Across from me, a young private slept badly, his helmet cradled in his lap as though it were something fragile. Whatever dreams troubled him were plainly no kinder than the waking world.

Outside, the land flattened and paled. Water crept closer to the tracks. Reeds bent beneath the wind's persistent hand. The sky pressed down until it felt no longer above us, but against us.

By the time I stepped down at the final station, the war felt both impossibly distant and uncomfortably near.

A military lorry waited, unmarked. Its engine ticked with faint impatience. The driver did not look at me when I climbed aboard, nor did he ask my name. He offered none of his own. We drove without speech as the road narrowed, then collapsed altogether, becoming no more than a scar through mud and shingle. Pools of standing water mirrored the sky so perfectly that it was impossible to tell where land ended and air began.

When the lorry stopped, the silence arrived with force.

Not emptiness — never that — but a hush so dense it felt deliberate. The sea breathed somewhere beyond sight. The wind slid across the land with a low, ceaseless sigh. Nothing else moved.

The driver gestured ahead. "Zeppelin's down there."

I thanked him. He was already reversing away, the lorry retreating like an animal that had delivered something dangerous and wished no further part in it.

I stood alone.

Orford Ness revealed itself grudgingly. A long, exposed spit of land, raw and stripped to its bones: shingle, scrub, salt-bleached grass. No trees. No shelter. The ground rolled gently but offered no comfort, each rise surrendering you more fully to the sky. I walked with my coat pulled tight, the wind needling through the seams, the air sharp with salt and decay.

Even before I saw it, I knew where the wreckage lay.

The air changed first — an undertone of oil and scorched metal, and beneath it something sweeter and fouler, a smell that unsettled the nerves. Then the shape emerged beyond a low ridge, and despite myself my breath caught.

The Zeppelin lay half-swallowed by the marsh, its enormous body split open, aluminium ribs exposed like the carcass of some vast, extinct creature. Torn fabric clung where fire had not finished its work, blackened and frayed, whispering faintly as the wind passed through. It had not shattered. It had settled. There was something almost careful about the way it had come to rest.

Someone had taken pains.

I circled the wreckage slowly, my boots sinking into the soft ground. Tracks marked the mud — soldiers' boots, several pairs, already blurring at the edges. Debris had been gathered and burned more thoroughly in places, as though fire itself had been directed rather than unleashed.

The Ness watched.

There was no mistaking the sensation; it was akin to a light but firm touch on the back, between the shoulder blades. The land was not empty. It was attentive. A place long accustomed to swallowing things had learned the virtue of patience.

I saw the drag marks then — shallow, broken, leading from the open belly of the wreckage toward a stand of reeds. I followed them. The smell deepened. The light thinned as I stepped inside the torn frame.

The interior was colder than I expected. Damp. The metal held the chill of the marsh and bled it into the air. Light fell through ruptured panels in narrow, colourless strips, flattening everything to a uniform grey. The structure shifted and complained as the wind worried at it, a low, laboured sound, like breath drawn through damaged lungs.

She lay where the frame dipped lowest.

For a moment, my mind offered the obvious lie — that she was another casualty of the crash, some unfortunate drawn into the machinery of war. But the body did not lie as bodies do when they are thrown by violence. She had been placed. Her limbs arranged. Her coat smoothed.

She was young. Too young for this place.

Her dark hair spread across the mud like ink in water. Her face was pale and unmarked. There was no soot on her skin, no burn damage to her clothes. The Zeppelin had not killed her.

I knelt, the mud seeping through my trousers, and examined her throat.

The bruising was deep and deliberate. Finger marks, unmistakable even in the cold. This had been done by someone who understood precisely how fragile the human body is — and exactly how much pressure is required to end it.

She had been murdered elsewhere.

The crash had merely been useful.

For a long moment I remained where I was, aware of my own breathing, of the way the wreckage seemed to lean inward, displeased by my intrusion. Outside, the wind dropped abruptly. The silence thickened until it rang.

I searched her pockets. Nothing. No papers, no letters. Only a plain ring on her finger, unadorned and unmarked.

Her hands were clean her nails trimmed short. A faint trace of lavender clung to her clothes, intimate and stubborn, refusing to yield to oil and rot.

This was not a woman of the marsh.

I moved deeper into the wreckage, guided more by instinct than reason. There were signs of violence here — a smear of dried blood on a strut, scuffed metal where someone had lost their footing — but it was old, its energy spent. Whatever had happened had concluded long before the Zeppelin fell.

The Ness had merely accepted what remained.

A break in the cloud allowed a blade of light to cut down through the torn hull, illuminating the body with sudden, pitiless clarity. Her face, peaceful in death, seemed almost to accuse me.

I covered her with my handkerchief. The gesture was small and futile, but it felt necessary. An acknowledgement, at least, that she had been seen.

When I stood, the Ness seemed to draw closer.

Land like this remembers. Especially places used and abandoned by men who believe themselves clever enough to erase their own footprints. Orford Ness had learned to keep what it was given — bones, secrets, lies.

I understood then why I had been sent without paperwork, without witnesses. This was not a crime meant to be spoken of loudly. The purpose was for it to be assimilated, becoming part of the extended, observant stillness.

I stepped back into the open air. The wind returned. The sea resumed its measured breathing. Somewhere, a bird cried once and fell quiet.

Behind me, the wreckage creaked softly, settling deeper into the marsh.

The war had come to Orford Ness not with guns or banners, but with a single dead woman and the hope that no one would look too closely. Someone had trusted the silence to protect them.

They were mistaken.

2

They kept him apart from the wreckage.

That was the first thing I noticed.

A temporary cordon had been thrown up near the lorry track — rope strung between posts driven hastily into the shingle, a boundary more symbolic than effective. Two guards stood there, stamping their feet against the cold, rifles slung, eyes fixed resolutely anywhere but the marsh. Beyond them, half-sheltered by a canvas lean-to, sat the German.

Johann Keller, according to the tag tied to his greatcoat.

He looked smaller than I had expected. Thin. Drawn in on himself as though the land were steadily compressing him. Though his hands were bound, the restraint was more a matter of custom than genuine necessity. He stared out toward the Ness, his gaze fixed not on the wreckage itself but on the low horizon beyond it, where sea and sky merged into a single, colourless band.

One of the guards intercepted me. "Prisoner's been talking nonsense, sir."

"So I'm told."

"Shock, most likely. The Zeppelin crew took a bad knock. Keeps saying things."

"Such as?"

The guard grimaced. "Says he saw a woman walking out of the marsh."

I did not react. I had learned long ago the value of stillness in moments like this.

"Alive?" I asked.

The guard snorted. "That's what he claims."

I nodded and stepped past him before he could say more.

Keller looked up as I approached. His eyes were pale, almost colourless, and too alert for a man supposedly lost to confusion. He watched me with careful intensity, as though weighing the danger I posed.

"You are not one of the guards," he said. His English was precise, lightly accented.

"No."

"Or the pilots."

"No."

"Then you are here because something has gone wrong."

I took that in. "Tell me what you saw."

His gaze flicked briefly toward the guards. They did not move, but their attention sharpened. Keller noticed. He lowered his voice.

"She was alive," he said. "She was walking. I saw her with my own eyes."

"Where?"

"Near the reeds. She came out of the fog."

Fog. Of course.

"When was this?"

"Before the crash," he said. "Shortly before."

I waited.

"We were losing altitude," he went on. "The storm had damaged the envelope. We were already doomed. I was at the observation window. I saw her then. A woman, alone, moving across the marsh as though she knew exactly where she was going."

"You are certain it was not a reflection? A trick of light?"

"No." His voice sharpened. "She was real."

"Did she look injured?"

"No."

"Frightened?"

"No."

That, more than anything, unsettled me.

"She was calm," he said. "That's what really got my attention."

I thought of the body, arranged with care.

"And after the crash?"

His mouth tightened. "After there was the fire. Smoke. Confusion. I did not see her again."

"But you believe the woman found in the wreckage is the same one."

"Yes."

"How can you be sure?"

"She wore a dark coat," he said. "And she walked without hesitation. Like someone who knew the ground."

I straightened slowly.

Behind me, one of the guards cleared his throat with exaggerated patience.

"That'll be enough, sir," he said. "Fellow's been at it all morning."

"Have you taken a formal statement?"

The guard exchanged a look with his companion. "Didn't seem necessary."

"Why not?"

"Because he's talking rubbish."

I turned back to Keller. "Did you tell anyone else what you saw?"

"Yes," he said. "Immediately. After we were taken into custody."

"And their response?"

A faint, bitter smile touched his mouth. "They laughed."

I let the silence stretch.

"You understand," I said eventually, "that the woman found in the wreckage was dead before the crash."

His head snapped up. "Dead?"

"Strangled."

The word landed heavily between us.

"That is impossible," he said at once. "I saw her walking."

"I don't doubt that you believe you did."

"No," he said. "You misunderstand me. I do not *believe* it. I know it."

The guards shifted, uncomfortable now.

"He's been like this," one muttered. "Fixated."

"Enough," I said quietly.

They fell silent.

I studied Keller more closely. His clothes were singed in places, his hands trembling faintly from cold or exhaustion, but his eyes remained clear. There was no wildness there. No eagerness. Only a controlled urgency, as though he feared that if he did not speak carefully, the truth itself might slip away.

"Describe her again," I said.

“She was young,” he replied. “Dark hair. She hurried, but without panic. As though she were late rather than afraid.”

Late.

“Did she look toward the airship?”

“Yes.”

“Did she react to it?”

“No.”

That was the detail that mattered.

I stepped back, allowing the guards to reclaim their sense of authority.

“We’ll take it from here,” one said, already dismissing Keller with his eyes.

“I expect you will,” I replied.

As I walked away, I felt it again — that subtle pressure between the shoulder blades. Not the Ness this time, but something human. A collective will, applied quietly, nudging the world back into the shape it preferred.

The guards were not merely unconvinced.

They were incurious.

That, I had learned, was rarely accidental.

I paused a short distance away and looked back. Keller had resumed his vigil toward the marsh, as though waiting for the land itself to confirm what he knew.

The wreckage lay silent behind him, settling deeper into the mud.

Somewhere between the two stood the truth, already being buried.

And someone was making very sure it stayed that way.

3

The Royal Flying Corps had attempted to civilise the Ness. They had done so with rope, canvas, timber, and optimism.

The installation lay inland from the wreckage, set back from the worst of the wind but not, I suspected, from its influence. A scatter of temporary structures clung to the shingle: hangars skinned in tarred cloth, timber sheds sunk unevenly into the ground, a mess tent bowed by weather and use. The flag flew, though without enthusiasm, its fabric snapping sharply as if offended by the air.

A man waited for me at the perimeter. He was stout, red-faced, and already apologetic in posture. His cap bore the insignia of the RFC; his boots were polished beyond necessity.

"Lieutenant Quirk," he said, offering a hand that was clammy with cold. "Captain Avery. We weren't expecting—"

"Few people ever are," I said, and stepped past him.

He fell into stride beside me at once, talking too quickly, as though silence might invite inspection.

"You'll have to excuse the state of things," he said. "Temporary arrangements. Experimental work. Nothing of interest, I assure you."

"Then we should get along famously."

We walked between two hangars where men were at work on a length of fabric stretched over a metal frame. A parachute, I realised—one of several—its pale silk already darkened in places by marsh damp. A corporal was barking instructions while another man climbed a ladder, hands shaking slightly as he fastened a line.

"Testing deployment times," Avery said. "Wind shear over open water presents unique challenges."

The corporal glanced at us, then away again, his mouth tightening.

Beyond the hangars, a crude tower had been erected from scaffolding and rope. At its top, a dummy hung suspended, limp as a drowned man. On a shouted signal, the rope was cut. The figure dropped, the parachute blooming a second too late the body striking the ground with a sound that carried.

No one laughed.

We moved on.

A row of cameras had been mounted on tripods near the edge of the marsh, their lenses hooded against glare. Cables trailed from them like roots, disappearing into a canvas-walled hut where a generator thudded and coughed.

"Aerial photography," Avery said. "Reconnaissance applications. Mapping. Intelligence."

I looked out over the Ness. The land offered no features worth mapping, no obvious landmarks to fix upon. It was all repetition and subtlety: shingle becoming reed, reed becoming water, water becoming sky.

"What are you hoping to see?" I asked.

He hesitated. "Patterns."

We passed a stretch of ground where nets had been thrown over wooden frames and painted in mottled greens and browns. Beneath them, mock artillery pieces lay half-concealed, their outlines deliberately blurred.

"Camouflage trials," Avery said, a shade more defensively. "Visibility from altitude."

"And from the ground?"

He did not answer at once.

A sharp crack split the air to our left. I turned in time to see a man flinch as a mounted machine gun spat a quick burst into the sandbank beyond. Another man peered through a sighting rig, adjusting dials with meticulous care.

"Sight calibration," Avery said. "Tracking moving targets."

"There's nothing moving out there," I said.

He followed my gaze, then looked away. "Not today."

The men avoided my eyes as we passed. Their movements were precise but brittle, as though rehearsed too often. I noted the way conversations dipped when I drew near, the way shoulders tightened. Engineers, not soldiers—men accustomed to problems that could be solved with numbers and patience. This place offered neither.

We reached a line of sheds set apart from the rest, their doors closed, their padlocks bright with newness. The surrounding ground was scuffed with recent traffic, boot prints pressed deep into the shingle.

"What's in those?" I asked.

Avery's smile faltered. "Stores. Instruments. Sensitive equipment."

"Sensitive to whom?"

He cleared his throat. "To the weather."

I stopped. The wind tugged at my coat. Somewhere behind us, the machine gun barked again, shorter this time, as if corrected.

"Captain," I said, "a woman was found strangled inside the wreckage of a German airship less than half a mile from here."

His eyes flicked, involuntarily, toward the marsh.

"Yes," he said. "We heard."

"And yet no one thought to mention it to the men?"

"They don't need to be distracted."

"By murder?"

"By speculation," he said quickly. "Morale is—fragile."

I studied him then. The red had drained from his face, leaving it mottled. He was not lying exactly. He was omitting. Carefully.

A group of villagers stood at the edge of the site, kept back by a length of rope and a pair of sentries who looked as though they had been drawn from the nearest pub and scrubbed just enough to pass muster. The villagers did not speak. They watched.

An older man with a fisherman's stoop leaned on a stick, his eyes narrowed against the wind. Beside him, a woman held a child's hand too tightly. Another woman stared at the ground, her mouth set, as though reciting something inwardly.

"Have you spoken to them?" I asked.

Avery grimaced. "Nothing useful. Rumours. Nonsense. They don't like the presence here."

"Why is that?"

"They say the Ness should be left alone."

"And what do you say?"

He gave a thin laugh. "I say the war doesn't afford us that luxury."

I approached the rope. The villagers did not retreat, but I felt the collective stiffening, the drawing inward. The older man met my gaze.

"You won't get answers from the land," he said without preamble.

"I'm not asking about the land," I replied.

He shook his head. "It listens all the same."

The sentry shifted, uncomfortable. "That'll be enough."

The man turned away, his duty done.

As we walked back, I felt it again—that pressure, subtle but insistent, urging me onward, away from certain questions. It was present in Avery's brisk explanations, in the engineers' lowered voices, in the villagers' refusal to elaborate. The silence here was not the natural hush of the Ness. It was curated.

We stopped near the locked sheds once more.

"Captain," I said, "how many people have access to those?"

"Authorised personnel only."

"Names."

He hesitated a fraction too long. "I can provide a list."

"You will."

He nodded, relief and resentment warring in his expression.

As I left the site, the Ness opened before me again, unbounded and indifferent. The experiments continued behind me—fabric snapping, engines coughing, metal striking metal—but their sounds diminished quickly, swallowed by the land.

Order was being imposed here. Lines drawn. Secrets locked away.

The Ness would outlast all of it.

It would remember what was brought to it, irrespective of whether the men present wanted it to.

4

They were building the wall when I found them.

The river ran thin and grey along the inland edge of the Ness, its course uncertain, braided where the land had not yet decided whether to hold it or let it go. The wall followed no elegant line. It was being forced into place, stone by stone—an assertion rather than a solution.

A dozen labourers worked there, boots sunk into mud, shoulders bent into the wind. They moved steadily and without conversation, passing stones hand to hand with the economy of men long practised in keeping their thoughts to themselves. The wall was not high—not yet—but already it cast a shadow out of proportion to its size.

I stopped some distance away.

The stones had been scavenged from elsewhere on the Ness. Old foundations. Broken revetments. Fragments of things once thought permanent. They bore the marks of earlier use: lichen scars, tool grooves, salt wear. Nothing here was new. Even the mortar smelled faintly of damp age, as though mixed with water that had served other purposes.

The men did not look at me at first.

They worked with the same care I had seen in the wreckage—deliberate, almost reverent. Each stone was placed, tested, adjusted. A mistake here would not announce itself. It would wait. It would settle.

A foreman stood apart, clipboard tucked under one arm, making marks at measured intervals. He glanced at me once, then away again, as though confirming something already decided.

I approached slowly. Boots shifted. A hammer paused, then resumed. One man wiped his hands on his trousers, leaving pale streaks of lime dust.

"You're not from the Corps," the foreman said at last.

"No."

"Then you'll want the site office." He gestured inland, toward where the RFC tents huddled against the wind.

"I'm interested in the wall."

He studied me more closely. "It's flood prevention."

"Is it effective?"

He shrugged. "That depends on what you think you're preventing."

I let that stand.

Work resumed, but something had altered. Movements grew fractionally tighter. Stones were handled with exaggerated care. The wall rose another inch—another claim laid against the water's quiet persistence.

One of the labourers caught my eye.

He was younger than the rest, slighter in build, his movements careful rather than strong. His hair was dark and neatly cut, his expression composed into something close to neutrality. When he straightened, I saw his hands were scarred—old burns, poorly healed.

He returned my gaze without challenge.

After a moment he set down his stone and stepped back, as though to ease his shoulders. He did not look at the foreman when he spoke.

"You should not stand too close," he said. His voice was soft. His English precise. "The ground is unstable."

"I've noticed."

He nodded once. "It always is. Here."

No one acknowledged the exchange. The work continued.

"Does the river often flood?" I asked.

"It remembers where it has been," he said. "Even when men tell it otherwise."

That word again—*remembers*. It had followed me from the wreckage, from the villagers' rope, from the omissions of men in uniform. I watched the water slide past the stones, untroubled, unconvinced.

"Your name?"

He hesitated—only briefly, but enough.

"Liang Wei," he said. "Sir."

"Mr Wei. How long have you been working here?"

"Long enough."

A hammer rang sharply as a stone slipped and was caught at the last moment. No one laughed. No one swore.

"What was here before the wall?" I asked.

Liang did not answer at once. His eyes flicked toward the foreman, who had turned his back and was making another mark on his clipboard.

"The river," Liang said at last. "And before that, other things."

"What sort of things?"

"Things not meant to last," he said. "But which did."

He bent and lifted another stone, setting it into place with care. I noticed then that he did not look at the wall as he worked. His attention was on the ground beneath it—on the way the mud shifted, the way the water darkened around the stones.

"You've seen the wreckage," I said.

It was not a question.

"Yes. We all have."

"And the woman?"

The hammering stopped.

Not all at once, but in stages, like breath being slowly withdrawn. One man straightened. Another wiped his hands again. The foreman looked up sharply.

Liang did not move.

"She was not of this place," he said carefully. "But she walked it as though she understood it."

I felt the weight of that settle.

"You saw her alive."

His fingers tightened on the stone.

"Yes."

The foreman cleared his throat. "That's enough."

Liang set the stone down gently. He did not look up.

"You should go, sir," the foreman said. "This is not a place for questions."

"Is it a place for answers?"

He did not reply.

I stepped back, offering the impression of retreat. The men returned to their work, though the rhythm had changed. It was more exact now. More guarded.

As I turned away, Liang spoke again, his voice barely carrying over the wind.

"The ground remembers," he said. "Even when people pretend they do not."

I did not look back.

I walked along the river for some distance, following its uncertain course. The wall diminished behind me, its purpose already beginning to feel provisional. Water has patience. So does land.

Ahead, the Ness lay open and unbroken, indifferent to the small violences imposed upon it. I thought of the woman's careful placement, of Keller's certainty, of cameras mapping patterns where none wished to be fixed.

Of men who had seen more than they could say.

By the time I reached the rise overlooking the wreckage once more, the light was failing. The Zeppelin's torn frame caught what remained of it, its ribs briefly illuminated before the colour drained away.

Below, the river continued its quiet work, testing the stones one by one.

I had the distinct impression that everything here was being watched—not with malice, but with memory. That nothing placed upon this land was ever utterly lost.

And that those who laboured upon it understood this far better than those who gave the orders.

I turned back toward the RFC camp, Liang Wei's words travelling with me.

The ground remembers.
So would I.

5

Captain Hargreaves received me as though I were an inconvenience already survived.

His office occupied one of the sturdier huts near the centre of the RFC installation its canvas walls reinforced with timber, its floor raised just enough to pretend at dryness. A stove ticked in the corner, radiating more sound than heat. The air smelled of boiled tea leaves—overworked and exhausted of flavour.

Hargreaves himself was a broad man whose neck appeared to grow directly from his shoulders. His uniform was immaculate. His moustache had been trimmed to regulation exactness, as though deviation might invite disorder. He did not rise when I entered.

"Lieutenant Quirk," he said, consulting a single sheet of paper that could not possibly contain anything of substance about me. "You're causing a certain amount of movement."

"Movement is preferable to stagnation," I said.

His eyes lifted briefly, assessing, then dismissed the remark as unproductive. "You've been speaking to my men."

"I've been observing," I said. "As instructed."

"That may be so," he replied, "but your observations are outpacing their usefulness."

I took the chair opposite him. The canvas wall behind me shifted faintly as the wind pressed against it, a reminder that nothing here—authority included—was as fixed as it pretended.

"The woman found in the wreckage," I said. "You've concluded she was a local."

Hargreaves folded his hands on the desk. His fingers were thick, square, well fed. "That's the most reasonable explanation."

"It's the most convenient."

He smiled thinly. "We are at war, Lieutenant. Convenience has its place."

"She wasn't burned," I said. "Not as the others were. There was no soot in her lungs. No damage consistent with a crash or with fire."

"Not everyone responds to trauma in the same way."

"She was strangled."

His smile held. "A tragic injury sustained during impact."

"With finger marks visible in the bruising pattern."

A pause. Brief, but real.

Hargreaves reached for his cup and took a measured sip of tea, as though giving the matter the respect it deserved. "You are not a medical officer."

"No," I said. "But I am not blind."

He set the cup down carefully. "The local explanation stands. A village girl. Curious, perhaps. Foolish. Caught too close to the wreckage."

"She was killed before the airship came down."

"You believe that."

"I know it."

His eyes hardened. “You are extrapolating beyond your remit.”

I felt again that pressure, familiar now—the resistance that met every attempt to push in the wrong direction. The Ness exerted it through land and silence. Men like Hargreaves exerted it through tone, through the careful application of authority.

“You’ve spoken to the villagers,” he continued. “They’re fond of stories. Always have been. This coast breeds them.”

“It also breeds memory.”

“That’s enough,” he said sharply. “The woman is dead. The cause is immaterial. The war will not pause while you indulge philosophical enquiries.”

I did not answer at once. My gaze drifted to the paperweight on his desk: a polished lump of flint mounted on a brass base. Taken from the Ness, no doubt. Even here, the land intruded.

“You have her effects,” I said finally.

Hargreaves frowned. “Excuse me?”

“Personal items recovered from the body.”

“They’re with the quartermaster. Nothing of note.”

“May I see them?”

“That won’t be necessary.”

“Then I will insist.”

For the first time his expression tipped fully into irritation. “You overestimate your authority, Lieutenant.”

“I underestimate your patience,” I said. “And your interest in accuracy.”

The silence that followed stretched, taut as wire. Outside, something metallic rang—hammer on frame, perhaps—and was abruptly silenced.

Hargreaves stood. He was taller than I had judged his bulk filling the narrow space. "Five minutes," he said. "And then you will leave this matter alone."

He led me to a smaller hut behind the central office, its door secured with a padlock that gleamed with recent use. Inside, a trestle table had been set beneath a hanging lamp. On it lay a small collection of items, each tagged and recorded with bureaucratic neatness.

A pair of boots, scuffed but well-maintained.

A plain woollen coat, damp-stained, the hem frayed from use.

A leather purse containing three coins, worn smooth by handling.

And a scrap of fabric, darkened at the edges, folded once and set apart.

"That's all?" I asked.

"That's all there was."

I picked up the purse first. It was soft with use. Inside, beneath the coins, lay a narrow strip of paper, folded and refolded until it was supple as cloth. I unfolded it carefully.

A name, written in a steady hand: **Eleanor**.

Nothing more.

"No surname?" I asked.

"Probably didn't see the need," Hargreaves said. "Locals seldom do."

The boots contradicted him. They were sturdy and practical, but not the sort sold in village shops. The stitching was tight. The leather supple. City work.

"She walked the marsh," Hargreaves said, watching me. "That doesn't make her remarkable."

"It makes her knowledgeable," I said. "Or desperate."

I lifted the coat next. Inside the lining, carefully stitched, was a small tear—repaired, not recently, but well. Someone had taken the time.

"She cared for her things," I said.

"Most women do."

"That's not what I mean."

I turned at last to the scrap of fabric.

It was silk or had been once. Pale. Fine. Patterned faintly with a repeating motif—flowers, perhaps, or stars. The edges were burnt and curled inwards, yet the centre remained soft. This was no working garment. No village dress.

"This didn't come from her coat."

"No," Hargreaves said. "It was found loose, near the body."

"From the airship?"

"Possibly."

I held it up to the light. Even darkened, it caught it differently the weave too delicate, too costly.

"She wore this under her coat," I said.

"You can't know that."

"Yes," I said. "I can."

Hargreaves stepped closer. "You are determined to make something out of nothing."

"I'm determined to see what you refuse to."

"The official record," he said, "will reflect an unfortunate local casualty. Nothing more."

"Then your record is a lie."

"That is an accusation."

"It's an observation."

Silence pressed in again, heavier now, no longer passive but enforced. I felt its weight settle between us.

"Five minutes," Hargreaves said again. "They're nearly up."

I replaced the items carefully. All but the scrap of fabric.

I folded it smaller and slid it into the inner pocket of my coat, the movement so ordinary it escaped notice. Hargreaves was watching my face, not my hands.

When we stepped back outside, the light had shifted. Afternoon had drained into something flatter, colder. The Ness stretched beyond the camp, unbroken, indifferent.

"You will leave this matter," Hargreaves said.

"I will leave this office," I replied. "Nothing more."

He snorted. "You're chasing ghosts."

"No," I said. "I'm listening to them."

He turned away, already finished with me.

I walked without direction at first, letting my feet carry me past the locked sheds, past the cameras and their blank, unblinking lenses. The engineers glanced up as I passed, then returned to their work, shoulders tight.

At the river wall, the labourers were still at it. The wall had grown by inches. The water tested it patiently.

Liang Wei glanced up as I approached. He said nothing, but his eyes flicked briefly to my coat, then away.

"She had a name," I whispered when the foreman's back was turned.

Liang nodded once.

"Eleanor."

He absorbed this without comment.

"She wasn't local," I went on. "You know that."

His jaw tightened. "Knowing is not the same as being allowed to say."

"You saw her."

"Yes."

"Where?"

"Near the old pilings," he said. "Where the river bends. She was walking fast."

"Alone?"

"Yes."

"Did she look afraid?"

"No."

That again. Calm. Purpose.

"She wore a fine dress," Liang said. "Under her coat."

I felt the scrap of silk warm against my chest.

"They told us she died in the crash," he continued. "They told us not to talk."

"Did anyone believe them?"

"Some did," he said. "Some needed to."

The foreman cleared his throat loudly. Liang returned to his stone.

I moved on, following the river as it curved back toward the wreckage. The air smelled of salt and iron. Gulls wheeled overhead, their cries thin and sharp.

At the rise, I stopped.

The Zeppelin lay as it had before—ribs exposed, frame sagging, fabric whispering. The Ness held it without comment.

I took out the scrap of dress once more, unfolding it carefully. Against the grey of the land, it looked almost luminous. A fragment of another life. Another world.

Eleanor.

I imagined her walking the marsh, coat pulled tight, silk hidden beneath wool. Late for something. Or running toward it.

Someone had thought the Ness would erase her. Swallow the truth along with the body.

They were mistaken.

I folded the fabric and returned it to my pocket.

6

I returned to the wreckage at dusk.

The light was already thinning, drawn out into long, colourless strands that failed to warm anything they touched. The Ness prefers this hour. Edges soften. Distances lie. The land loosens its outline and invites error.

The Zeppelin lay where I had left it, half-sunken, patient. Its ribs caught what tiny light remained, a pale lattice against the darkening marsh. Torn fabric whispered as the wind passed through it, the sound of paper handled by gloved hands.

I stood for a moment before approaching, listening.

No voices. No engines. Only the sea, breathing somewhere beyond the shingle, and the soft, complaining creak of metal settling further into mud. The silence was no longer unfamiliar. It felt deliberate—an accomplice rather than a warning.

I stepped inside.

The interior had changed since my last visit, though nothing visible had shifted. Absence will do that. Without daylight the space felt narrower, the air heavier, as though the wreckage were drawing itself closed. My breath sounded loud to my own ears. I slowed it, matched it to the land.

I manoeuvred, torch hooded, letting the beam skim rather than strike. The floor sloped gently toward the marsh where the structure had settled. I knew where the body had been. I did not look that way.

Instead, I followed the frame toward the gondola.

It sat lower than the rest, more intact. Scorched, but not consumed. The windows were cracked, opaque with soot. The door hung open, bent on its hinges, as though forced rather than blown.

That alone gave me pause.

Crash damage has a grammar of its own. Violence leaves patterns—chaotic but consistent. This door had been opened with intention.

I stepped closer.

Inside, the air was stale and trapped. The smell of oil and burned insulation lingered, overlaid with something else: paper. Old, dry. Faint, but unmistakable once recognised.

I closed the door behind me.

The gondola was cramped, its fittings buckled but recognisable. Control panels sagged on torn mounts. A chair lay overturned, its straps snapped. There were signs of haste here—scratches where tools had been dragged free, compartments left ajar.

Someone had been in a hurry.

I worked methodically, letting habit guide me. Open compartments. Check beneath seats. Run fingers along seams where things might be tucked rather than stored. This was not my first search of a place that did not wish to be searched.

It was behind a loosened panel near the floor that I found them.

At first I took it for insulation—cloth bundled and wedged into the cavity. I reached in and pulled gently. The bundle came free with surprising ease.

Paper.

Not German.

British.

My torch caught the edges first: squared, deliberate, too neat for anything improvised. I unfolded the top sheet carefully, aware of how brittle it felt, how easily history can be destroyed by impatience.

Typed. Official. Marked.

Not intended for enemy eyes.

I read slowly, translating not language but implication. Coordinates. Schedules. Names reduced to initials. References to coastal installations. Experimental trials. Supply routes. Not everything resolved at once, but enough did.

This was intelligence.

British intelligence.

The cold settled properly then—deep, precise.

I thumbed through the rest. More documents, some handwritten, others typed. A map, folded to near transparency along its creases. A partial cipher sheet, legible enough to be dangerous. All of it wrapped against moisture, concealed with care, placed where only someone familiar with the gondola's layout would think to hide it.

This was not the work of a panicked crewman acting alone.

Someone had put these here.

The Zeppelin had not merely fallen onto British soil.

It had been carrying something out of it.

I sat back on my heels, the metal cold even through my coat, and let that truth settle. The Ness creaked softly, as though adjusting itself around the new understanding.

Eleanor had been calm. Purposeful. Seen walking the marsh without hesitation. She had known the ground. She had known where she was going.

Late, Keller had said. Not afraid.

I closed my eyes briefly, assembling the shape of it.

Documents gathered elsewhere. Moved quietly. A handover planned under cover of weather and war. The Zeppelin as courier, not a weapon. The crash was an interruption, not the design.

And when it went wrong, I thought of her body, placed with care. Hidden, not discarded. Of the scorched silk, too fine for the marsh, concealed beneath wool.

She wasn't supposed to die in this place.

Her departure was planned.

I gathered the documents and re-wrapped them, returning them to the cavity exactly as I had found them. This was not evidence to be paraded. Not yet. Not here.

I eased the panel back into place and stood.

The gondola felt smaller now, crowded with unspoken things. I opened the door and stepped back into the wreckage. The sky beyond had darkened to slate. The first stars showed, thin and remote.

I paused at the threshold and looked back once.

The Zeppelin said nothing.

Neither did the land.

That, I was learning, did not mean consent.

Outside, the wind had strengthened, moving through the torn fabric with renewed insistence. The wreckage breathed—damaged lungs labouring against the night. I followed the frame back toward the open hull, careful where I placed my feet.

Near where the body had been, I stopped.

The marsh had already reclaimed the space, water creeping inward, smoothing the disturbance. The Ness does not hurry. It does not need to.

I took the scrap of silk from my pocket and held it up in the torchlight. It caught again, faintly luminous, stubborn in its refusal to become ash. I folded it and returned it to my coat.

Not evidence, exactly.

A reminder.

As I stepped back into the open air, the camp lights flickered in the distance—yellow, constrained, temporary. Human light, imposed upon a place that would outlast it.

Someone in that camp knew what the Zeppelin had carried. Someone had known Eleanor's role, or at least her value. Someone had decided that when the plan failed, silence would serve better than explanation.

Captain Hargreaves's voice returned to me, flat and certain.

A local girl. Caught in the crash.

It was a lie that required effort. Coordination. Rehearsal.

The guards' incuriosity. The engineers' unease. The locked sheds. The wall was forced against the river. All of it pointed the same way.

Containment.

I left the wreckage and began the long walk back, the Ness opening around me, indifferent to my conclusions but not, I thought, to the truth buried beneath them.

The ground remembers, Liang Wei had said.

So does paper.

And so, now, did I.

7

The labourers finished the rest of the work.

Not deliberately. Not all at once. The truth seldom arrives with ceremony. It gathers instead at the margins, among those accustomed to being overlooked.

I found them at the wall again, the river running low and grey beside their work. The stones had risen another foot since my last visit. Water tested the base patiently, sliding around the mortar as though taking notes.

The men worked without speaking. From a distance, the rhythm looked almost peaceful. Up close it was something else—careful, guarded, each movement weighed.

Liang Wei saw me first.

He did not wave. He did not smile. He shifted his stance subtly, placing himself between me and the foreman's line of sight. It was a small thing, easily missed. I did not miss it.

"You returned," he said.

"I had more questions."

He inclined his head. "That is rarely a good reason."

"For some," I said. "Others rely on it."

We stood together for a moment, watching the water. Wind carried the smell of salt and damp stone. Somewhere inland, an engine coughed, then fell quiet.

"You spoke to Captain Hargreaves," Liang said.

"Yes."

"And?"

"He insists the woman was local," I said. "Killed in the crash."

Liang's mouth tightened, almost imperceptibly.

"That is not what they told us at first," he said.

I turned toward him. "What did they tell you?"

He did not answer at once. One of the other labourers glanced up, then away. Something passed between them—brief enough to be denied, clear enough to be understood.

Liang spoke without looking at me.

"They told us to say nothing," he said. "Before they told us what had happened."

I waited.

"There was a woman," he went on. "Before the airship fell. She was seen."

My pulse slowed. That happened sometimes, at moments like this—the body preparing itself.

"Seen where?"

"On the Ness," he said. "Walking."

"When?"

"Two days before the crash. Perhaps three. Days are not kept carefully here."

"Who saw her?"

Liang tipped his chin, barely.

"All of us," he said. "At different times."

One of the men set down his stone and straightened. He was older than Liang, his hair threaded with grey, his face weathered by places that offered endurance without reward. He wiped his hands on his trousers and stepped closer.

"She walked early," he said, his English rougher, less practised. "When the mist still lay on the ground."

"Alone?"

"Yes."

"Lost?"

He shook his head. "No. She walked as if she knew where she was going."

That again. Calm. Purpose.

"She wore a coat," Liang said. "Dark. Plain."

"And beneath it?"

Liang glanced at the older man. The older man nodded once.

"A finer dress," he said. "Light. It showed when the wind caught it."

"How do you know?"

"She crossed near the river bend," he said. "Where the ground dips. The coat opened."

Silk, then. Or something close enough to matter.

"Did she speak to any of you?"

"No," Liang said. "But she looked at us."

"How?"

"Not like someone asking for help," the older man said. "Like someone checking."

Checking what, I did not ask.

"Did she come from the direction of the wreckage?"

"No," Liang said. "From inland."

That settled it.

Eleanor had not drifted onto the Ness in the confusion after disaster. She had been there before the Zeppelin ever appeared in the sky. She had learned the ground. Used it.

"She was here more than once," Liang said quietly. "We think."

"How can you be sure?"

"The ground remembers," he said.

I let that stand.

"When did they tell you to forget her?"

The older man gave a short, humourless sound. "The morning after the crash."

"Who told you?"

"A man from the camp," Liang said. "Not a soldier. An engineer."

"Did he give his name?"

"No."

"But you recognised him."

"Yes."

"From where?"

Liang hesitated.

"From the sheds," he said at last.

The locked sheds.

"Did he say what would happen if you spoke?"

"He did not need to," Liang said.

The foreman's cough carried across the site then—deliberate, pointed. Liang stepped back and took up his stone. The older man did the same.

Before turning away, Liang spoke again, low enough that only I could hear.

"She was not a mistake," he said. "She was part of something."

I nodded.

"So were they," I said. "All of you."

He met my gaze for a moment, then returned to his work.

I left the wall and walked back toward the camp, the Ness opening around me, its silence altered now by what I knew. Eleanor had been present on this land before the fire before the crash. She had moved with intent. She had been observed—and then erased.

Or so they had hoped.

I took the long way, skirting the outer perimeter of the RFC site. From there, the sheds stood apart from the rest of the installation, aligned with faint deliberation, their padlocks catching the light. New locks. Recent hands.

I did not approach them.

I watched who did.

Two engineers entered within half an hour. Without hesitation, as though accustomed to the privilege. Neither lingered. Neither appeared to carry anything away.

Access, then. Controlled, but not rare.

The documents in the gondola had not placed themselves there.

Someone with knowledge of the airship's interior had done so—someone who understood concealment, and the danger of being seen too often in the same place. Someone who believed the Ness would swallow what it was given.

A sentry intercepted me as I turned away, posture rigid.

"Lieutenant," he said. "You're wanted."

"By whom?"

"Message just came through," he said. "From London."

That had been inevitable.

They cleared space for me in the communications hut. The generator hummed steadily. The air smelled of oil and ozone. The operator did not meet my eyes as he handed over the paper.

The message was brief. Typed. Unadorned.

Return to London at once. Your presence at Orford Ness is no longer required.

Unsigned.

But the weight behind it was unmistakable.

I folded the paper and slipped it into my pocket, next to the scrap of silk. It felt heavier now, as though it had absorbed something of the moment.

"Any reply, sir?" the operator asked.

"Yes."

I took a pencil and wrote beneath the message, my hand steady.

Investigation incomplete. Evidence discovered. Will report in person.

I handed it back.

Outside, the wind had shifted. Light thinned toward evening. Beyond the ridge, the wreckage lay quiet, holding what remained of its secrets.

London wanted silence.

The Ness was unsympathetic to what London wanted.

And neither, I had decided, did I.

8

The world grew more restricted the next day.

Not abruptly. Not in any way that could be named at first. The situation grew more tense, as is typical when elements are drawn together by an unseen influence, with paths converging, possibilities diminishing, and silences taking on a distinct character and intent.

I felt it before I understood it.

The camp was awake earlier than usual. Men moved with a purpose that did not invite questions. Conversations ended when I drew near. A sentry who had nodded to me the day before now asked to see my papers again, apologetic but firm. The generators ran longer. The sheds remained locked.

Containment, I thought.

The word returned unbidden, carrying weight with it.

I went first in the gondola.

The Ness lay pale under early light, mist clinging low to the marsh, softening distances and blurring edges. The wreckage rose out of it like a memory that refused to be dismissed. I approached with care, senses tuned to minor disturbances—the kind that betray recent passage.

There were fresh boot prints near the gondola door.

Not soldiers.' Not labourers.' The tread was finer the spacing deliberate. Someone had been here since my last visit.

I did not go inside.

Not yet.

Instead, I circled the wreckage, letting habit assemble its muted inventory. Who could access the gondola without challenge? To hide documents where neither fire nor water could reach, one would need intimate knowledge of its interior.

The pilots were accounted for—dead or under guard. The sentries lacked familiarity. The labourers had never been permitted near it.

That left the engineers.

Men who moved freely between sheds and hangars. Men who worked with structures and tolerances, with panels and cavities. Men accustomed to labouring unseen.

I thought of the two I had watched the evening before, entering the locked sheds without pause. I did not yet know their names, but I knew their posture now—the ease of men who did not expect to be stopped.

The Ness watched as I turned away, its silence neither helpful nor obstructive, only attentive.

Back at the camp, the tightening announced itself more clearly.

Captain Hargreaves was waiting.

Not in his office this time. He stood outside it, flanked by two men I had not seen before. Their uniforms were neat, their expressions unmarked. One carried a leather satchel.

"Lieutenant," Hargreaves said. "We need to speak."

"So you keep saying."

"This is no longer a request."

The man with the satchel stepped forward. "Authority has been granted to secure all materials pertaining to the incident."

"By whom?" I asked.

Hargreaves did not answer.

I chose my next words carefully. "You're late."

His eyes flickered briefly. "Excuse me?"

"I've already seen what you're trying to protect."

Silence followed—not the Ness's silence, but the human kind. Calculating. Adjusting.

"Then you understand," Hargreaves said slowly, "why this cannot continue?"

"What cannot continue," I replied, "is pretending the woman died by accident."

"The woman is dead," he said. "Her motives are irrelevant."

"They aren't," I said. "And neither is her name."

That did it.

Hargreaves nodded once. The man with the satchel stepped closer.

"We'll need whatever you've taken," he said. "Notes. Objects. Anything removed from the site."

I thought of the scrap of silk, folded warm against my chest. Of the documents returned carefully to their hiding place. Of Eleanor Selwyn's name, written small but steady.

"You'll need a warrant," I said.

"We have authorisation."

"From London?"

"From where it matters."

I smiled thinly. "Then you'll forgive me if I ask to see it."

The man hesitated. Hargreaves did not.

"This is your final warning, Lieutenant."

I stepped past them.

For a moment, I thought they might stop me. They did not. That, too, was information.

They were not ready.

Not yet.

I went instead to the quartermaster's hut.

The ledger was not where it should have been.

Absence has a shape of its own. I followed it to Dr Marwood.

He occupied one of the smaller sheds near the rear of the site, its door half open, the smell of oil and chalk drifting out. Inside, diagrams covered the walls—cross-sections of engines, airflow studies, measurements reduced to lines and figures that pretended neutrality.

Marwood looked up as I entered, startled.

"Lieutenant," he said. "You shouldn't be here."

"I know," I said. "That's why I am."

He swallowed. "This isn't—"

"About you?" I finished. "No. It's about what you wrote."

The ledger lay open on the bench between us.

My expectations regarding its size were not met; it was smaller. Unpretentious. The cover was frayed, and the spine was split from being handled frequently. The pages were dense with entries—dates, initials, figures that meant nothing in isolation.

And there it was again.

Containment.

Constantly in the margin and in the same hand. Sometimes followed by a number. Sometimes by a letter in place of a name.

"What does it mean?" I asked.

Marwood closed the ledger carefully. Too carefully.

"It's a technical term," he said. "Experimental notation."

"For what?"

"For limiting exposure."

"Exposure to what?"

He did not answer.

I took the ledger from him. He did not resist.

Tucked between two pages was a folded sheet of paper.

Handwritten.

Eleanor Selwyn's hand.

I recognised it at once.

Her notes were precise, unsentimental. Names. Dates. Movements between sheds. A list of questions asked and never answered. At the bottom, underlined twice:

Marwood. Hargreaves. Shed Three.

I looked up.

"You knew her," I said.

Marwood's face seemed to collapse inward, as though something long held had finally given way.

"She came looking for her brother," he whispered.

"Who was he?"

"Thomas Selwyn. Engineer. Assigned to experimental munitions trials."

"Missing," I said.

"Murdered," Marwood corrected. "Inside Shed Three."

The air altered, subtly, as if the room had shifted its weight.

"She knew," he went on. "She worked it out. That's why she came back. Not to run. To finish it."

"To expose it."

"Yes."

"And the Zeppelin?"

"She realised what it was being used for," he said. "A way out. A way to move information without drawing attention."

"She wasn't a courier," I intoned.

"No," Marwood said. "She was the architect."

I closed the ledger.

Outside, boots crunched on shingle.

"They're coming," Marwood said.

"I know."

I slid the ledger under my coat, next to the silk.

"They'll call it containment," he said. "They always do."

"I know," I replied. "But they're running out of ground."

I stepped back into the light.

The Ness waited.

And for the first time since I had arrived, I understood fully what it was holding.

9

I learned Arthur Selwyn's name the way most inconvenient truths are learned—by accident, and too late to be ignored.

It appeared in the camp register as though it meant nothing at all.

I had gone to the records hut under the pretence of confirming personnel assignments, my presence still tolerated because it had not yet been expressly forbidden. The clerk inside was young, conscientious, and exhausted. He worked with the careful diligence of someone who believed that order itself was a moral act.

He did not look up when I spoke.

"Engineer Selwyn," I said. "Arthur Selwyn."

His pencil paused.

"Not currently assigned," he said.

"I know."

A faint frown creased his brow as he turned a page. "Transferred," he offered.

"When?"

Another pause. Longer this time.

"Before the crash," he said. "Some weeks ago."

"To where?"

He hesitated, then shook his head. "That information isn't kept here."

"Is it kept anywhere?"

He looked up then, properly. "Sir—"

"Just tell me what the book says."

He exhaled, resigned, and turned the register toward me.

Arthur Selwyn was listed under **Engineering Personnel – Experimental Division**. The entry was neat, unremarkable. Beside his name, in a different hand, was a brief annotation:

Removed from site. Duties concluded.

No date. No destination. No signature.

"That's it?" I asked.

"That's all there is," the clerk said.

"How often do engineers simply vanish?"

He considered the question too literally. "They don't vanish, sir."

"No," I said. "They don't."

I closed the book and stepped back. The space beyond the hut felt suddenly narrower, as though the camp itself had drawn a breath and chosen not to release it.

Duties concluded.

A phrase that suggested finality while explaining nothing at all.

I did not return immediately to the wall or the wreckage. Instead, I walked the perimeter of the experimental site, counting steps, watching patterns. Shed One: calibration. Shed Two: propulsion. Shed Three—always locked, always guarded more carefully than the rest.

Always absent from conversation.

Shed Three was where Eleanor Selwyn's notes had pointed.

And now Arthur Selwyn's absence did the same.

I found Dr. Marwood later that afternoon, seated alone in the mess tent. His tray lay untouched. He looked smaller than he had the day before, as though something essential had been removed.

"Arthur Selwyn," I said.

He closed his eyes.

"So you've found him," he murmured.

"I've found where he stops existing," I said. "Explain that."

Marwood folded his hands together, knuckles whitening. "The official explanation," he said carefully, "is that he was reassigned."

"To where?"

"An inland facility," he said. "The name changes depending on who's telling the story."

"And the unofficial one?"

He hesitated.

"Arthur was asking questions," he said at last. "The wrong ones. About materials. About trial results that didn't match the reports."

"And this concerned whom?"

"Everyone," he said. "And no one. That's how it works."

"Did he leave of his own accord?"

Marwood shook his head. "Arthur wouldn't have left Eleanor without telling her."

That alone told me more than the register ever could.

"She came looking for him," I said.

"Yes."

"She didn't come to grieve."

"No."

"She came to investigate."

"Yes."

"And she succeeded."

Marwood looked at me then, properly. "That's why she died."

We sat with that while the tent filled and emptied around us. Cutlery scraped. Men laughed too loudly at a joke that did not deserve it. Life, continuing.

"What happened in Shed Three?" I asked.

Marwood did not answer.

"Arthur Selwyn was last seen entering that shed," I went on. "And never seen leaving it."

Marwood's gaze flicked toward the tent opening, where a sentry stood outlined against the light.

"Experiments fail," he said carefully. "Men are injured. Records are amended."

"Bodies don't simply disappear."

"They do," he said. "Here."

"And the official explanation?"

A short, humourless sound escaped him. "Containment."

Of course.

The word that made lies sound procedural.

"He was declared unstable," Marwood continued. "Mentally compromised by the work. Removed for treatment."

"No physician signed that," I said.

"No."

"No facility received him."

"No."

"And yet that version is being repeated."

"Yes."

I stood.

"Who authorised it?"

Marwood did not answer.

"Who benefits from it?"

He looked away. That was answer enough.

I left the mess and walked toward Shed Three.

I had no intention of entering it. I knew better. Instead, I watched who went in and out—and when.

Two engineers. Always the same two. Always together. Always at times when no trials were scheduled.

One of them I recognised. Tall. Ink-stained fingers. A habit of watching the river instead of the work. I had seen him at the wall once, standing apart.

The other was younger, sharper, his confidence a shade too deliberate.

Men accustomed to secrets.

I committed their names to memory rather than paper. Paper could be taken.

Memory, less easily so.

It was near dusk when the second approach came.

This time it was not Hargreaves.

A man in civilian clothes intercepted me near the edge of the camp. His manner was polite. His tone regrettably firm.

"Lieutenant Quirk," he said. "You have outstayed your welcome."

"According to whom?"

"According to London."

He produced a document, properly signed this time. I read it once, then folded it carefully.

"And if I refuse?"

His smile was thin. "Then matters will escalate."

"They already have," I said.

He agreed.

"Arthur Selwyn," I said instead. "Where is he?"

The man's smile faltered—for a fraction of a second.

"His case is closed."

"It isn't," I said. "It's been buried."

"Be careful, Lieutenant."

"I am."

I stepped past him, aware of the eyes on my back.

The world was closing now, unmistakably so. Routes narrowing. Options thinning. But the shape beneath the pressure—the truth they were trying to compress—had at last come into focus.

Arthur Selwyn had not disappeared.

He had been removed.

Eleanor Selwyn had discovered this.

And in doing so, she had made herself dangerous.

The Ness had not killed her.

Men had.

And they were very keen that no one else remember.

Unfortunately for them, the ground already had.

And so had I.

10

I had been circling the truth for days before it allowed itself to be named.

That, I was learning, was its preferred method. It did not present itself whole. It revealed edges first. Shadows. Negative space. Only when enough had been removed did the shape beneath become undeniable.

Arthur Selwyn had not vanished.

He had been erased.

And Eleanor had come to Orford Ness to understand why.

I confirmed it in the quietest way possible.

Not through confrontation. Not through confession. Through paperwork—misfiled, incomplete, and quietly resistant, as though even the paper itself wished to be left alone.

The Selwyn name appeared again in the medical ledger, not where it should have been, but where someone had attempted to hide it among irrelevancies. A note appended to an intake record. A reference in a margin, crossed through and rewritten. I followed it patiently, the way one follows a river that refuses to be straight.

Selwyn, E.

Next of kin notified.

Not *wife*.

Not *mother*.

Next of kin.

I sat with that for a moment, the wind rattling the canvas above my head.

Eleanor Selwyn.

Arthur's sister.

The simplicity of it struck harder than revelation usually does. No grand conspiracy required. No elaborate explanation. Just blood, loyalty, and the kind of persistence that does not ask permission.

She had not come to the Ness by accident.

She had come because Arthur had stopped coming home.

I found the rest in her notes.

They were not hidden particularly well, which was its own kind of disguise. Tucked into the lining of the coat. Folded small. Written in a neat, economical hand that wasted nothing. Eleanor Selwyn had not written like a woman recording her grief. She had written like someone building a case.

Dates.

Times.

Names reduced to initials.

Shed numbers.

She had learned the rhythms of the place quickly. Who worked late. Who arrived early. Which sheds were locked when they should not have been. Which men avoided questions by answering too quickly.

And always—*Shed Three.*

Arthur had been assigned there shortly before he disappeared.

Arthur had raised concerns there.

Arthur had entered it, according to the men who worked nearby, and had not been seen leaving.

There was no accident recorded.

No injury logged.

No body recovered.

Only *containment*.

The word appeared again and again in Marwood's ledger, always in the same hand, always applied after a correction had been made. Figures altered. Results amended. Exposure reduced.

Containment did not mean safety.

It meant silence.

Eleanor had understood that.

She had come to Orford Ness not to mourn her brother, but to finish what he had started. To find out what had been done to him—and why.

She had walked the Ness in the days before the crash, mapping it with her feet, watching from the margins. The labourers had seen her. The guards had not looked. The engineers had noticed—and remembered.

She had not been hiding.

She had been *waiting*.

Waiting for the moment when information could move.

Waiting for the Zeppelin.

The airship had not been her escape route.

It had been her deadline.

I realised that as I stood outside Shed Three, watching the guards shift their weight against the cold. The door was newer than the others. The padlock heavier. The precautions excessive.

This was not a place one secured to keep things in.

It was a place one secured to keep things *from getting out*.

Arthur Selwyn had discovered something inside this shed that could not be allowed to surface. Eleanor had discovered that he had been killed for it.

And when she realised the Zeppelin was being used to move information quietly—under the cover of enemy action—she had adapted.

She had not planned to flee Britain.

She had planned to expose it.

The crash had not stopped her.

It had only accelerated her timetable.

Someone had realised that too.

Someone had understood what Eleanor Selwyn represented—not a courier, not a witness, but a threat.

She had been silenced before she could leave.

Strangled.

Placed.

Hidden.

And explained away as a local girl who had been foolish enough to wander too close to a burning machine.

Captain Hargreaves's voice returned to me, precise and incurious.

A local. Caught in the crash.

It was not just a lie.

It was a *rehearsed* one.

I felt the world tighten again as I put the pieces together.

Not metaphorically.

Physically.

A sentry moved closer to the shed door. Another appeared at the end of the track, pretending to study a clipboard. The camp had learned the shape of my attention and was responding accordingly.

I was no longer merely inconvenient.

I was dangerous.

I returned Eleanor's notes to my pocket and stepped away from the sheds, conscious now of eyes that did not trouble themselves to hide. Somewhere behind me, a door closed. Somewhere else, a conversation ended.

Containment, in practice.

London would not wait much longer.

Neither, I suspected, would whoever had authorised Arthur Selwyn's removal.

The dead woman in the wreckage had not been an accident.

She had been an interruption.

And interruptions, I had learned, were corrected quickly.

I walked back toward the Ness as the light began to fail, the wind rising again from the sea. The land lay open before me, indifferent to names and explanations, but not, I thought, to truth.

Arthur Selwyn had been killed inside Shed Three.

Eleanor Selwyn had discovered that.

And for that, she had been murdered.

The war would absorb this easily, if allowed. Files would be closed. Ledgers corrected. Men reassigned.

Containment would be declared complete.

Unless someone refused to let the ground forget.

I stopped at the rise overlooking the wreckage and took out the scrap of silk one last time. It fluttered faintly in the wind, pale against the grey.

Not a token.

Not evidence.

A promise.

The world was tightening now.

And I was no longer merely looking.

I was in it.

10

I had been circling the truth for days before it allowed itself to be named.

That, I was learning, was its preferred method. It did not present itself whole. It revealed edges first. Shadows. Negative space. Only when enough had been stripped away did the shape beneath become undeniable.

Arthur Selwyn had not vanished.

He had been erased.

And Eleanor had come to Orford Ness to understand why.

I confirmed it in the quietest way possible.

Not through confrontation. Not through confession. Through paperwork—misfiled, incomplete, and quietly resistant, as though even the paper itself wished to be left alone.

The Selwyn name appeared again in the medical ledger, not where it should have been, but where someone had attempted to bury it among irrelevancies. A note appended to an intake record. A reference in a margin, crossed through and rewritten. I followed it patiently, the way one follows a river that refuses to be straight.

Selwyn, E.

Next of kin notified.

Not *wife*.

Not *mother*.

Next of kin.

I sat with that for a moment, the wind worrying the canvas above my head.

Eleanor Selwyn.

Arthur's sister.

The simplicity of it struck harder than revelation usually does. No grand conspiracy required. No elaborate explanation. Just blood, loyalty, and the kind of persistence that does not ask permission.

She had not come to the Ness by accident.

She had come because Arthur had stopped coming home.

I found the rest in her notes.

They were not hidden particularly well, which was its own kind of disguise. Tucked into the lining of the coat. Folded small. Written in a neat, economical hand that wasted nothing. Eleanor Selwyn had not written like a woman recording grief. She had written like someone building a case.

Dates.

Times.

Names reduced to initials.

Shed numbers.

She learned the rhythms of the place quickly. Who worked late. Who arrived early. Which sheds were locked when they should not have been. Which men avoided questions by answering too quickly.

And always—*Shed Three*.

Arthur had been assigned there shortly before he disappeared.

Arthur had raised concerns there.

Arthur had entered it, according to the men who worked nearby, and had not been seen leaving.

There was no accident recorded.

No injury logged.

No body recovered.

Only *containment*.

The word appeared again and again in Marwood's ledger, always in the same hand, always applied after a correction had been made. Figures altered. Results amended. Exposure reduced.

Containment did not mean safety.

It meant silence.

Eleanor had understood that.

She had come to Orford Ness not to mourn her brother, but to finish what he had started. To find out what had been done to him—and why.

She had walked the Ness in the days before the crash, mapping it with her feet, watching from the margins. The labourers had seen her. The guards had not looked. The engineers had noticed—and remembered.

She had not been hiding.

She had been *waiting*.

Waiting for the moment when information could move.

Waiting for the Zeppelin.

The airship had not been her escape route.

It had been her deadline.

I realised that as I stood outside Shed Three, watching the guards shift their weight against the cold. The door was newer than the others. The padlock heavier. The precautions excessive.

This was not a place secured to keep things in.

It was a place secured to keep things *from getting out*.

Arthur Selwyn had discovered something inside this shed that could not be allowed to surface. Eleanor had discovered that he had been killed for it.

And when she realised the Zeppelin was being used to move information quietly—under the cover of enemy action—she adapted.

She had not planned to flee Britain.

She had planned to expose it.

The crash had not stopped her.

It had only accelerated her timetable.

Someone had realised that too.

Someone had understood what Eleanor Selwyn represented—not a courier, not a witness, but a threat.

She had been silenced before she could leave.

Strangled.

Placed.

Hidden.

And explained away as a local girl foolish enough to wander too close to a burning machine.

Captain Hargreaves's voice returned to me, precise and incurious.

A local. Caught in the crash.

It was not merely a lie.

It was a *rehearsed* one.

I felt the world tighten again as the pieces settled.

Not metaphorically.

Physically.

A sentry shifted closer to the shed door. Another appeared at the end of the track, pretending to study a clipboard. The camp had learned the shape of my attention and was responding accordingly.

I was no longer merely inconvenient.

I was dangerous.

I returned Eleanor's notes to my pocket and stepped away from the sheds, conscious now of eyes that did not trouble themselves to hide. Somewhere behind me, a door closed. Somewhere else, a conversation ended.

Containment, in practice.

London would not wait much longer.

Neither, I suspected, would whoever had authorised Arthur Selwyn's removal.

The dead woman in the wreckage had not been an accident.

She had been an interruption.

And interruptions, I had learned, were corrected quickly.

I walked back toward the Ness as the light began to fail, the wind rising again from the sea. The land lay open before me, indifferent to names and explanations, but not, I thought, to truth.

Arthur Selwyn had been killed inside Shed Three.

Eleanor Selwyn had discovered that.

And for that, she had been murdered.

The war would absorb this easily, if allowed. Files would be closed. Ledgers corrected. Men reassigned.

Containment would be declared complete.

Unless someone refused to let the ground forget.

I stopped at the rise overlooking the wreckage and took out the scrap of silk one last time. It fluttered faintly in the wind, pale against the grey.

Not a token.

Not evidence.

A promise.

The world was tightening now.

And I was no longer merely looking.

I was in it.

11

The day began with a mistake that was not a mistake at all.

A sentry stopped me before I reached the track that led from the huts toward the marsh. He was one I had seen before—same cap, same apologetic eyes—but his posture had altered. He stood as though instructed, as though he had been given a shape to occupy.

"Lieutenant," he said, and did not step aside.

I let my hand rest lightly on the papers in my pocket—not for comfort, but for measure. The message from London. My reply beneath it. Eleanor Selwyn's name in my own hand. The scrap of scorched silk folded smaller than a handkerchief. All of it had weight now. Not physical. Moral.

"What is it?" I asked.

He swallowed. "Orders, sir. You're to report to Captain Hargreaves at once."

"Again?"

He did not smile. He did not apologise. He repeated the instruction, as though repetition itself might become authority.

"At once."

I could have gone. I could have walked into Hargreaves's office and let him do what men like him do best—fill the air with certainty until doubt begins to look unreasonable. But the camp had shifted in the night. The friction in every exchange was no longer the land's indifference. It was organisation. A hand at the back, steering.

The world tightening.

"I'll go in a moment," I said. "I need to see the wreckage first."

His eyes flicked, once, inland.

"No, sir."

That single syllable was the newest thing on Orford Ness.

I looked past him. The track lay pale with frost, leading toward the low ridge and the marsh beyond. Nothing moved there. The Ness offered no witness. It never did. It merely remembered.

"Who gave you those orders?" I asked.

He hesitated. "Captain. And... there's a gentleman from London."

Of course.

London had stopped being a presence and become a person.

I nodded, as though conceding, then turned away—not toward Hargreaves's office, but toward the hangars where the morning's work had already begun.

If the camp intended to contain me, it would do so by narrowing my options until I chose the wrong path without realising. That is how containment works: it asks nothing. It simply removes.

Men moved in purposeful clusters. A corporal shouted. A generator coughed and settled into a steady thrum. The air smelled of oil and damp canvas, and beneath it the same metallic tang I had come to associate with this place—iron leached from the land itself, as if the Ness bled slowly and without complaint.

Avery spotted me and made an instinctive motion to intercept, then thought better of it. He lingered at the edge of a group of engineers, speaking too softly, eyes refusing mine.

I kept walking.

The parachute tower stood against the low sky like a crude gallows. Yesterday it had been an experiment. Today it felt like a rehearsal.

A dummy had been hoisted again to the top, limp in its harness. A parachute pack sat against its back, the silk folded into a neat promise. Men worked the ropes with the careful briskness of those who did not want to be the one holding the line when something went wrong.

I stopped at the edge of the cordon.

A corporal barked, "Clear," and the rope snapped free.

The dummy dropped.

For a heartbeat, the parachute did nothing. Then, as if reconsidering, it began to open—hesitating, snagging—before blooming into a half-formed canopy that collapsed on itself.

The dummy struck the ground hard.

The sound travelled. It always did out here because the land offered nothing to catch it.

No laughter followed. No swearing. Only quick, disciplined movement as men converged, lifting the dummy with more haste than concern, glancing not at the damage but at who might have been watching.

I had been watching.

Avery approached with a face arranged into something like competence.

"Testing is ongoing," he said quickly. "Wind variability. Silk tolerances. There are—"

"That was sabotage," I said.

His eyes widened, then narrowed, as though selecting the correct expression.

"Lieutenant, I assure you—"

"That pack wasn't packed," I said. "Not properly. A man doesn't forget his work like that."

Avery's gaze slid sideways, toward a pair of engineers standing a little apart. One was tall, with ink-stained fingers even at this hour. The other was younger, his hair cut close, his confidence too carefully held.

The two I had seen near Shed Three.

The tall one looked away at once. The younger did not. He held my gaze for a fraction of a second too long, then offered a polite, meaningless nod.

It was the kind of courtesy one extends before closing a door.

"What are their names?" I asked Avery, without looking at him.

Avery's throat bobbed. "Engineers," he said, as if that were sufficient.

"Their names."

He licked his lips. "Hollis," he said at last. "And Pritchard. Mr Hollis and Mr Pritchard."

Pritchard.

I turned the name over, once, and set it aside. It was the first solid thing I had been given in hours.

Avery was still speaking—weather, materials, tolerances—but his words no longer mattered. The parachute had failed at the exact moment the camp began to tighten around me. That was not coincidence. It was demonstration.

We can make accidents, it said. *We can correct interruptions.*

I left Avery to his explanations and walked toward the photography hut.

The camera rigs stood in a row at the marsh edge, lenses hooded, tripods braced like limbs against the wind. Cables ran from them into the hut where plates were developed and logged, where images became intelligence and intelligence became leverage.

If something had been seen, it would be here.

Inside, the hut was warmer, dense with chemical smell and the faintly sweet, unsettling odour of solution. A young technician looked up sharply, then down again at once.

He had the look of a man standing between obedience and fear.

"Lieutenant," he said. "You're not—"

"I'm not meant to be anywhere," I said. "Show me yesterday's plates."

"They're classified."

"So is murder."

His eyes flicked to the curtain dividing the developing space from the rest of the hut. Beyond it, someone moved. A footstep. A pause.

"Who's here?" I asked.

"No one," he said too quickly.

I drew the curtain aside.

A man stood there with a leather satchel and the kind of expression that never belonged to the land. Civilian clothes, cut too well. A face clean-shaven and unremarkable by design.

London, given a body.

"Lieutenant Quirk," he said pleasantly. "We do keep meeting."

"You're early," I said.

He smiled. "You're slow."

The technician stood rigid beside his trays, eyes fixed on nothing.

"I've been authorised," the man went on, "to secure materials relevant to the incident."

"Then you'll forgive me if I ask to see the authorisation."

He produced a document. Properly signed. Properly stamped. The paper itself looked heavier than it ought to have been, as though weight could be manufactured through ink.

I read it once. The wording was broad enough to be a net.

"Everything relevant," I said.

"Yes."

"And you define relevance."

"I don't," he said. "London does."

A movement behind him. Pritchard stepped into the hut as if he belonged there. Hollis followed, slower, eyes on the floor.

Suspects did not multiply all at once. They converged.

The noose did not appear. It tightened.

Pritchard gave the London man a brief nod, almost imperceptible, then turned to me with the same careful politeness he had offered outside.

"Lieutenant," he said. "You're causing disturbance."

"And you're arranging accidents," I said.

Hollis flinched. Pritchard did not.

"That parachute pack was faulty," I said. "Who packed it?"

"The corporal," Pritchard said.

"Who supervised?"

Pritchard's smile held. "You're not on the trial staff."

"I'm on the truth."

The London man stepped slightly between us, as though softening the exchange.

"This doesn't need to become unpleasant," he said. "We would prefer cooperation."

"Prefer," I echoed.

"Yes. Prefer."

A polite word. Behind it, the machinery.

"You'll be returning to London," he said. "Immediately."

I glanced at the technician's trays. A plate lay drying near the edge, its surface still wet enough to catch the light.

"Before I go," I said, "I'd like to see what your cameras have captured."

"That won't be necessary."

"No," I said. "It will."

Pritchard's eyes narrowed, a fraction.

"You misunderstand your position."

I let the silence stretch, long enough to remind them I had learned its uses before arriving here.

Then I moved—not toward them, but toward the plate.

The technician made a sound, half protest, half warning.

My fingers hovered above the wet surface.

And I saw it.

Not clearly—not enough for certainty—but the shapes were there: the low ridge, the line of the river, the wall under construction, and farther out, near the marsh edge, a figure in a dark coat. Too small to show a face. Distinct in posture.

A woman, alone.

And beside her—two men.

They were not labourers. Their stance was wrong for work. They stood too still.

Even frozen, intent shows.

The technician's breath caught. The London man's expression tightened for a fraction of a second before smoothing again.

Pritchard stepped closer, too smoothly.

"That's enough."

He reached for the plate.

I lifted it first, holding it by the edge, letting the chemical sheen run in a thin line across the surface.

"What day is this?" I asked.

The technician hesitated. Then, quietly: "Three days before the crash."

Eleanor had been here. Before the crash.

Not a local girl wandering into disaster.

A planned presence.

A meeting.

The London man's voice sharpened. "Lieutenant—"

I angled the plate. The taller man's posture—shoulders hunched, head angled down—was familiar.

Hollis.

The shorter stood too straight. Even blurred, there was something drilled about him.

Pritchard.

"Take it from him," the London man said.

The order was quiet.

That chilled me most.

Violence shouted is still human. Violence spoken softly is administrative.

Hollis moved first, hesitated, then stopped. His eyes went to Pritchard, seeking instruction.

Pritchard did not look at him. He looked at me.

In that moment I understood something else.

Hollis was not the man who did things.

He was the man who watched them happen.

Pritchard was the one who corrected interruptions.

The procedural collapse is never dramatic. It is simply the moment the pattern aligns.

I stepped back toward the hut's rear door.

Pritchard lunged—not with panic, but calculation.

The plate slipped from my fingers.

Not dropped—released.

It struck the floor and shattered, glass bursting into bright, wet fracture.

The technician cried out.

Pritchard froze, staring at the ruin as if he had lost not evidence, but control.

"You've made this difficult," the London man said.

"I've made it visible."

Then I was out the back, into the wind.

Footsteps followed.

Two sets. One lighter, quicker. One heavier, reluctant.

I ran.

Not blindly. Not toward the Ness, which would swallow me as readily as secrets. Toward the sheds.

Shed Three.

The place locked to keep things from getting out.

The padlock gleamed in the flat light.

A sentry stood nearby, shifting his weight. When he saw me, his hand moved toward his rifle.

"Lieutenant," he called. "Stop."

Behind me, Pritchard's voice carried, calm and clipped. "He's to be detained."

Detained.

Not arrested.

Contained.

The word returned, a shadow over the ground.

I slowed, raising my hands slightly.

Then I did the one thing men like Pritchard never plan for.

I spoke to the sentry as if he were a man.

"Do you know what's in that shed?" I asked.

He blinked. "No, sir."

"Do you know what happened in it?"

His mouth opened, then closed.

Pritchard reached us, breath steady, face composed.

"This is finished."

"For you."

His eyes flicked to my coat. To the pocket where silk, paper, and names lived.

The London man arrived next, not running—merely arriving.

"This is your final opportunity to cooperate."

"And if I don't?"

"Then matters will be resolved without you."

The sentry looked between us, lost, eager for instruction.

I could have fought. I could have run. Either would have given them the justification they wanted.

Instead, I said, "Fetch Dr. Marwood."

Pritchard's eyes tightened.

The London man's expression did not change, but the air did. A recalculation.

"Dr. Marwood is occupied."

"Dr. Marwood," I said again, louder. "Now."

The sentry hesitated, then—because he was young and still believed in procedure—ran.

For a moment, no one moved.

Pritchard's gaze held mine with irritation.

"You don't understand."

"I understand perfectly," I said. "You've used the war to hide your work. The crash to hide the body. The Ness to hide the truth."

"And you?" he asked. "What have you used?"

"Memory," I said. "It's harder to confiscate."

Dr. Marwood arrived within minutes, breathless, hair slipping loose under her cap.

Not *he*, I realised—not as my assumptions had shaped her, but *she*: Elspeth Marwood, chief engineer, the mind behind half the calculations that kept this place upright. The surname had disguised her. The camp had encouraged it.

She took in the scene at once.

"Lieutenant," she said. "What have you done?"

"What you should have done," I said. "Stopped pretending this is about weather and equipment."

Pritchard cut in. "Doctor, the Lieutenant is interfering with classified work. He is to surrender any materials he's taken."

Marwood's gaze sharpened. "Materials?"

"The ledger," the London man said gently. "Any notes. Any items recovered."

Marwood's eyes went to my coat.

I saw something pass through her expression—fear, yes, but not for herself.

"You wrote 'containment' in your margins," I said softly. "Over and over."

Marwood's face tightened. "Lieutenant—"

"What does it mean?"

"Experimental notation," she said automatically, the echo of a story told often enough to be usable.

"And Arthur Selwyn?"

Pritchard shifted. Barely.

The London man glanced at him.

Marwood went still.

"Who told you that name?"

"Your ledger," I said. "And Eleanor Selwyn's notes."

At Eleanor's name, Marwood's composure fractured. A breath caught. A blink too slow.

"She wasn't a local," I said. "She was Arthur's sister. And she was investigating his disappearance."

The sentry stared, the word *sister* doing more damage than *documents* ever could.

Pritchard spoke quickly. "Doctor, do not engage. He has no standing."

Marwood looked at him as though seeing a familiar machine and recognising, at last, what it had been built to do.

"What have you been doing, Pritchard?" she asked.

"My duty."

"And what is your duty?"

"To keep this work from compromising the war effort," he said, without hesitation. "To prevent panic. To prevent exposure."

Containment.

He did not say the word, but it sat behind his teeth.

"And Eleanor?" I asked. "Was she compromising the war effort?"

Marwood's voice dropped to a whisper. "She came because Arthur stopped writing. Stopped sending money home. Stopped existing."

The London man sighed, almost regretfully. "Doctor, this is beyond your discretion."

Marwood's eyes moved—to the shed door, the padlock, the sentry, the men standing too close.

Shifting alliances are not announced. They are decided in silence.

She turned to me. "Give me the silk."

I stared. "What?"

"The scrap," she said. "If they search you, they'll find it. If they find it, they'll have the excuse they want."

Pritchard's eyes narrowed.

The London man's smile returned, gentle and predatory. "Doctor, I must insist—"

Marwood stepped closer, lowering her voice. "Lieutenant, you're in the wrong part of the machine. Let me move you."

Trust was no longer moral. It was tactical.

I slid the silk into her hand without looking.

She folded it into her glove as if it were nothing at all.

"Now," she said, louder, turning to the London man, "you may search him."

They did.

Hands on my arms. Firm. Professional. No striking. No shouting. Procedure applied to flesh.

They found the London message. They found my reply.

They did not find the silk.

Pritchard watched with an expression that suggested he already knew the result and disliked it anyway.

"You'll be escorted to the transport," the London man said. "You will return to London."

"And if I don't?"

"Then the next attempt will not be administrative."

I looked at Marwood.

She held my gaze for a fraction of a second, then glanced—quickly, subtly—toward the photography hut.

A direction.

An opening.

The midpoint reversal is not courage. It is the moment you realise there is no safe way to remain passive.

Observation had brought me here.

It would not get me out.

I nodded as if conceding.

Then, as the men shifted their grip to guide me, I acted in the margin.

I stepped sideways, hard, wrenching one arm free long enough to drive my shoulder into the sentry nearest the shed door. He stumbled—not hurt, merely surprised—and in that moment the world widened by an inch.

I ran.

Not toward the Ness.

Toward the photographs.

Behind me, a shout.

Pritchard's voice, clipped: "Stop him."

The London man's voice, quieter: "Not if you can avoid damage."

And Marwood's voice—so soft I almost missed it—carried on the wind like warning and promise together.

"The ground remembers," she said.

The Ness did not care who hunted whom.

It only kept what it was given.

And I, now, intended to give it something other than silence.

12

I did not slow until the wind burned my lungs and the sound of pursuit thinned into distance.

The photography hut squatted ahead of me like a confession that did not wish to be made. Canvas walls. Blacked-out windows. A door that resisted just enough to suggest it had learned to expect hands like mine. I slipped inside and pulled it closed, holding my breath until the latch settled with a dull, final click.

For a moment there was only darkness and the chemical smell—sweet, metallic, unsettling. The world reduced to breath and listening.

No footsteps.

Not yet.

I moved by memory. Tables. Trays. The hanging red lamp that turned skin into something other than human. I drew it on and the room bled into view, shadows thickening rather than retreating. The plates lay where I had last seen them, lined like promises that had learned patience.

The technician was not there.

That absence mattered.

I went to the rack and lifted the first plate, holding it by the edge. The image was still wet enough to catch the light and bend it. I tilted it until the land resolved: the low ridge, the wall, the river's uncertain line.

And beyond—farther out, where the marsh surrendered to water that pretended to be empty—a shape that did not belong.

Not wreckage.

Not accident.

Geometry.

Straight lines where erosion should have ruled. Angles too deliberate for chance. A pale rectangle cut into the coast, its edges disguised from the ground by scrub and false contour, its face turned away from casual eyes.

The cold arrived then—clean, exact.

I moved to the next plate.

And the next.

The geometry repeated. Different heights. Different light. Different days. The camera had not known what it was seeing; it had only obeyed. The land had been patient. The lens had been honest.

A restricted naval installation.

Hidden not by walls, but by omission. The kind of place that does not exist until it must—and then only to those who already know.

Dry docks masked as tidal pools. A slipway whose angles refused the language of water. Scars in the sea where hulls had met steel and been swallowed again by tide and silence. The faint suggestion of rails beneath weed-dark water, leading nowhere a fisherman would ever choose.

I did not need a label.

I did not need a legend.

This was what someone had tried to smuggle out of Britain.

I set the plate down and reached for the ledger.

Dr. Marwood's book lay where she had left it, the cover worn to softness, the spine split by use. I opened it to the page I had memorised and read the word again, as though it might change if stared at long enough.

Containment.

There it was, in the margin. And again. And again.

Numbers followed it. Letters. Cross-references that meant nothing alone and everything together. Dates that aligned with the plates. Tide tables, lightly pencilled. Weather notes. Wind direction. Exposure reduced.

Not safety.

Silence.

I turned pages until my fingers learned the pattern. The ledger did not explain. It assumed knowledge. It trusted the reader to understand the cost and to accept it.

That was Marwood's failing—if failing it was. Not malice. Not profit.

Compliance.

I matched entries to images until the shape beneath them stood clear.

The installation was experimental. Provisional. Not meant to last. Not meant to be seen. Its existence compromised the war effort precisely because it mattered. It was being tested, measured, corrected. And someone—inside the machinery—had decided that if Britain could not protect it from knowledge, it would be protected by absence.

By removal.

By the slow, careful movement of information out of the country under the cover of enemy action.

The Zeppelin had been convenient.

The crash had been catastrophic.

Eleanor Selwyn had understood this faster than anyone intended her to.

She had come to the Ness not as a courier, but as a cartographer of guilt. She had learned the land. The rhythms. The tides. She had watched the cameras and understood what they could see that men refused to look at.

She had read Marwood's ledger.

And then she had set a clock.

I lifted the next plate and stopped.

This one was different.

The angle was higher. The light harsher. The timing precise. The installation was clearer here, its edges sharper, its lines refusing disguise. And near the edge of the frame—almost lost against the marsh—a figure stood in a dark coat, the wind opening it just enough to betray what lay beneath.

Eleanor.

She was not alone.

Two men stood with her. One tall, shoulders curved inward as though attempting to shrink from his own shadow. One shorter, posture rigid, exact. They were not labourers. They were not guards.

They were engineers.

Hollis and Pritchard.

The photograph did not capture their faces. It did not need to. It captured what mattered: proximity. Timing. Intent.

This had not been chance.

This had been arranged.

I felt the moment settle—not as surprise, but as confirmation. Truth does that when you have already paid for it. It does not astonish. It aligns.

The door rattled.

Once.

Then again.

"Lieutenant," a voice said, calm and measured. "Open the door."

London.

I slid the plate into the ledger and closed the cover gently, as though not to startle it. I tucked both beneath my coat, the weight familiar now, earned.

The door shook harder.

"Last opportunity," the voice said. "We can do this cleanly."

Clean.

The word scraped.

I crossed to the rear of the hut and lifted the canvas flap. Cold air rushed in, sharp as rebuke. Beyond it, the marsh lay low and open, the light already thinning toward evening.

The Ness waited.

I went out backward, then turned and ran.

Not toward the water. Not toward the wall.

Toward the ridge.

Shots cracked behind me—warning shots, I thought, because anything else would have admitted too much. The sound skittered across the land and fell away, swallowed without comment.

The Ness does not echo.

It absorbs.

I ran until the hut vanished and the camp lights blurred into something like memory. My boots sank and rose and sank again. The land took its due in inches and breath.

At the ridge I stopped, chest burning, and looked back.

From here, the installation could not be seen. The Ness had learned that lesson well. From here, the war looked ordinary again. Canvas and timber. Men moving with purpose. Lines drawn and redrawn.

Containment.

I turned the ledger to the back and found Eleanor's notes folded small and exact. I read them once more, not because I needed to, but because reading is a form of remembering.

She had written with restraint. With care. She had written as someone who knew that words outlive bodies.

Arthur was right.

They will not stop unless forced.

If I do not leave, make it visible.

She had not intended to escape.

She had intended to expose.

The Zeppelin had been her deadline, not her route.

The crash had taken her before she could deliver the truth whole, but it had not destroyed it. The photographs existed. The ledger existed.

And now, so did I.

I took out the scrap of silk, pale against the darkening land, and pressed it into the ledger's spine as a marker.

Not evidence.

A promise.

Below me, the tide turned. The river tested the wall again. The Ness continued its quiet work, indifferent to rank and seal and instruction.

Somewhere behind me, men would be calculating how much force could be applied without consequence. Somewhere else, London would be deciding how best to fold this away.

They were too late.

Containment depends on ignorance.

Truth, once seen, acquires momentum.

I turned from the ridge and began the long walk east, the ledger heavy at my side, the photographs warming beneath my coat, the land opening before me with the patience of something that has always known how this ends.

The ground remembers.

And now, so would the war.

13

The motorbike failed without drama.

No explosion. No skid. No sudden violence to announce itself. The engine simply lost its voice, coughed once, and settled into a silence that felt deliberate. I coasted to a stop on the shingle road, boots skimming loose stone, the headlamp cutting a narrow tunnel through the dark.

For a moment I stayed where I was, hands on the grips, listening.

The Ness answered with nothing.

I tried the ignition again. The engine turned, obedient but hollow, as though the connection between intention and result had been quietly severed. I dismounted and crouched beside the bike, lifting the lamp to peer beneath the casing.

It did not take long.

The fuel line had been sliced clean through—not torn, not worn, but cut. Neat. Considered. Whoever had done it had known exactly how far I would travel before the engine starved.

An accident would have been messier.

This was instruction.

I straightened slowly and looked back along the road. The shingle track lay pale under the moon, curving away toward the distant camp lights, which now seemed very far off. The wind had dropped, leaving the land in a hush so complete it pressed against the ears.

The bike would not be ridden again tonight.

I took the ledger from my coat and shifted it beneath my arm, adjusting the weight. The photographs rested against my ribs, warming with my body heat. Evidence, now. Not merely proof, but burden.

I began to walk.

The shingle was treacherous in the dark, each step uncertain, every stone eager to turn an ankle. I kept my pace measured, listening to the rhythm of my own movement, careful not to rush.

Panic makes noise.

Noise invites attention.

The Ness did not need encouragement.

The sense of being watched arrived gradually.

Not as fear, at first, but as awareness. A subtle tightening between the shoulders. A slight adjustment of posture. The instinct that tells you the land has begun to count your steps.

I stopped.

Nothing moved.

The marsh lay low and black on either side, reeds whispering faintly where the breeze found them. Above, the sky was clear, the stars sharp and indifferent. Ahead, the road vanished into darkness.

I walked on.

After a hundred yards, I heard it—a sound just out of time with my own footfall. Not close enough to place. Not loud enough to confirm. The suggestion of movement rather than movement itself.

I did not turn.

Predators learn quickly which gestures invite pursuit.

Instead, I altered my pace slightly, slowing just enough to test the echo of my steps. The sound adjusted with me. Still distant. Still careful.

Someone was there.

Not rushing. Not closing. Simply keeping me company.

The thought that it might be Pritchard crossed my mind, then settled uneasily beside its opposite. Pritchard did not follow. He directed. He set things in motion and waited for the correction to complete itself.

This was someone else.

Or several someone's.

The road dipped, then rose, cresting a low ridge that overlooked the marsh. From here, the wreckage should have been visible, its torn ribs pale against the dark. Instead, the Ness had swallowed it whole. Even catastrophe could be hidden, given time.

I stopped again, pretending to adjust the strap of my bag.

The sound behind me stopped too.

That confirmed it.

I let my hand rest on the ledger, feeling the unevenness of the pages beneath the cover, the slight ridge where Eleanor's notes were folded inside. For a moment I considered turning back—confronting whatever followed me, forcing the issue into the open.

But that was not how this place worked.

The Ness did not reward confrontation.

It rewarded patience.

I walked on.

The road narrowed near the inland edge of the marsh, the shingle giving way to firmer ground. The smell changed here—less salt, more damp earth, iron seeping up from beneath. My breath fogged faintly in the cool air.

Another sound, closer now. A stone displaced. The soft crunch of weight shifting.

I did not quicken my pace.

Fear announces itself.

Purpose does not.

Instead, I spoke.

Not loudly. Not sharply. Just enough to disturb the silence.

"You can come closer," I said. "I'm not running."

The words vanished into the dark without reply.

A few steps later, the sound returned—now on both sides of the road. Not one presence, then. Two. Possibly more. They moved with the land, not against it, their steps absorbed where mine rang.

I began to understand.

This was not an attempt to take the ledger.

Not yet.

It was a reminder.

You are not alone.

You are being measured.

You can be reached.

The road bent toward the river. The low wall emerged as a darker line against darker ground. Water slid past the stones with quiet insistence, testing each one in turn. The wall held—for now.

I stepped off the road and onto the grass, angling toward the riverbank. If I was to be followed, I would choose where.

The sound behind me shifted accordingly.

I crouched near the water and pretended to retie my boot, lowering my centre of gravity, letting the dark settle. The river reflected the stars in broken fragments, never holding any of them for long.

"Arthur Selwyn," I said quietly, not entirely sure why.

The name felt heavier here, closer to the ground.

No answer.

But the sound behind me faltered.

Just for a moment.

That was enough.

Whoever followed me knew the name. Knew its weight. Knew why it mattered.

I rose and continued along the river, keeping the wall to my left, the marsh to my right. My shadow stretched and broke across the stones, fractured by moonlight.

I began to think then not of escape, but of sequence.

The bike had been disabled before I left the camp. That meant access. Time. Certainty of my route. Someone had assumed I would rely on speed, assume movement itself was protection.

They had not planned on the walk.

The walk changed things.

The dark does not belong to those who plan by daylight.

As the river curved away, the sound behind me thinned, then split. One presence peeled off, circling wide. Another remained.

Testing.

I stopped again, slowly this time, and turned my head just enough for moonlight to catch my face.

"You'll have to do better than this," I said. "I'm still breathing."

A mistake.

The reply came at once—not in words, but in motion. Displaced air. The snap of a reed breaking close enough to feel.

I stepped sideways, instinct overtaking thought, and something passed through the space where I had been—a weight, fast and controlled. I felt it rather than saw it, the brief absence where a body had been.

I fell hard, shoulder striking stone, pain flaring white before receding into something manageable. The ledger skidded from my grasp and landed in the grass a yard away.

That mattered more than the pain.

I rolled and reached for it at the same time someone else did.

Our hands brushed.

The touch was gloved. Cold.

I twisted, dragging the ledger back toward me, and kicked blindly. My heel connected with something solid. A grunt answered—sharp, restrained.

The figure retreated, quick as it had come, dissolving into the dark without pursuit.

Silence rushed in to fill the space.

I lay still, counting breaths, listening for return.

Nothing.

Whoever it was had not been sent to retrieve the truth.

They had been sent to show me how easily it could be lost.

I pushed myself upright and retrieved the ledger, tucking it back beneath my coat. My shoulder throbbed, but nothing felt broken. The body keeps its own accounts.

I stood and looked back along the road.

The Ness offered no sign of what had passed. It never did. It kept only what it was given—and exacted payment in other ways.

I resumed walking, slower now, more cautious, favouring the firmer ground near the wall. The camp lights were closer, their glow dull and unreliable, but they marked direction.

Containment had failed.

That was the truth of it.

If they could not take the evidence cleanly, they would make the cost of carrying it unmistakable.

As I walked, I understood something else.

The walk was not an inconvenience.

It was instruction.

Every step impressed itself into the land. Every pause altered the night. Whatever followed me would leave its trace, however briefly, in a place that did not forget.

The ground remembers.

So do men.

By the time I reached the edge of the camp, the first suggestion of dawn was threading the sky—pale, undecided. The hour when secrets feel briefly heavier, before daylight pretends they were never there.

I did not look back again.

There would be time for that later.

14

Daylight makes liars bolder.

In the dark, men move carefully. They listen. They weigh consequence. In daylight, they explain. They account. They issue orders and call it order. What was done at night becomes, by morning, something that must be made reasonable.

I returned to the camp as the sun climbed reluctantly over the marsh, pale and unimpressed by what it revealed. The Ness looked unchanged. It always did. That was its advantage. Men aged here. Structures sagged. Truth shifted. The land did not.

They were already explaining my injuries.

A corporal intercepted me before I reached the central huts, his expression arranged into something concerned but incurious.

"Took a spill, sir?"

"On the road."

He nodded, satisfied. The words had shape. They could be written down.

A medic glanced at my shoulder, prodded once, then twice. "Nothing broken. Strain, maybe. You'll feel it tomorrow."

"Good," I said. "I'd hate to miss anything."

He did not smile.

Orders were being issued everywhere I looked. Men stood in pairs, not speaking. A sentry I had not seen before guarded the communications hut. Another had been posted near the photography rig. The parachute tower stood empty, its gallows dismantled for the day. Yesterday's failure had been absorbed, reclassified, rendered provisional.

Containment, by daylight.

Captain Hargreaves made himself visible. Deliberately so. He stood near the hangars speaking to a cluster of officers, his voice pitched just low enough to require proximity. When he saw me, he did not break stride. He finished his sentence, nodded once, and dismissed them.

"Lieutenant," he said. "You're looking worse for wear."

"The road is unforgiving."

"So is disobedience."

We stood there, the wind threading between us, the Ness listening.

"London has clarified matters," he went on. "You are to cease your investigation immediately. You will return to London today."

"I've already declined."

His mouth tightened. "That was before."

"Before daylight?"

"Before patience wore thin."

I glanced past him, toward the marsh. "You've been busy."

"Busy men win wars."

"Busy men bury mistakes."

He stepped closer. "Careful."

"With what?"

"With accusations."

"I'm past them," I said. "I'm working with facts."

He held my gaze. For a moment, I thought he might strike me. Instead, he smiled—thin, administrative.

"You're overtired," he said. "And you're beginning to see patterns where none exist."

"Then you'll have no objection to me speaking to Keller again."

The smile faltered. Only slightly.

"The German?" he said. "He's in no fit state."

"He's been in the same state since I arrived," I said. "The difference is what he's saying."

Hargreaves hesitated.

"Keller is being transferred," he said at last. "For interrogation elsewhere."

"When?"

"Immediately."

"Then now seems ideal."

He studied me, recalculating. Then, with visible reluctance, he nodded to a guard.

"Five minutes," he said. "And then this ends."

It never did.

Keller sat where I had last seen him, hands still bound, though loosely. He looked worse in daylight. Grey. Drawn. But his eyes were clear—clearer than most on the Ness.

"You came back," he said.

"Yes."

"Then it was true," he said. "The woman."

"It means you saw something," I replied. "Tell me again. Slowly."

The guards shifted, listening without appearing to.

"She was not running," Keller said. "Not hiding. She was angry."

That was new.

"Angry with whom?"

He swallowed. "With one of your officers."

The word landed heavily.

"Describe him."

"British uniform," Keller said. "Not flying corps. Older. Confident. He stood as if the ground belonged to him."

I thought of Hargreaves. Then dismissed it. Keller shook his head slightly, as if hearing the thought.

"Not him," he said. "Another. He did not shout. He did not need to."

"Where did you see them?"

"Near the marsh edge," Keller said. "Close to the river. She stood facing him. He stood angled away, as if already finished."

"Did you hear what was said?"

"No. But I saw her gesture. She struck his chest with her hand. Once. Hard."

I pictured Eleanor Selwyn then—not the careful figure in the photographs, not the body in the wreckage, but a living woman, furious enough to risk exposure.

"She was not afraid," Keller went on. "She was demanding something."

"What happened next?"

"He said something," Keller said. "Quietly. After that, she stopped moving. Not because she agreed. Because she understood."

Understood what, I did not ask.

"They parted," he said. "She walked inland. He walked toward the camp."

"Did anyone else see this?"

Keller shook his head. "If they did, they did not look."

"And you?"

"I was watching," he said. "From above. From your sky."

The guard behind him shifted. "That's enough."

"Did you tell anyone?" I asked quickly.

"Yes," Keller said. "After the crash. I said I saw her alive. I said she argued with an officer."

"And?"

"They told me I was confused," he said. "Smoke. Reflection. Guilt."

His voice dropped. "They told me it would be easier if I stopped talking."

"Do you think they'll blame you for her death?"

He met my gaze. "I think they already have."

I stood.

"That's all," the guard said, eager now.

"No," I said. "That's enough."

As I walked away, Keller called after me.

"She knew she was in danger," he said. "But she came anyway."

"So did you," I replied.

He almost smiled.

The camp had rearranged itself by the time I returned. Orders read. Movements restricted. Hollis stood alone near Shed Two, pale, hands empty. Pritchard was nowhere to be seen.

That absence mattered.

I found Dr. Marwood in the open now, deliberately so, near the photography hut. Her hair was pinned more tightly than before. Her expression had settled into something like resolve.

"They're separating us," she said quietly. "Isolating variables."

"Which one frightens them more?" I asked.

She did not answer at once. Then, "Pritchard."

"And Hollis?"

"He follows," she said. "He records. He survives."

"And you?"

She met my gaze. "I complied," she said. "Until compliance stopped protecting anything I recognised."

"You knew about Arthur."

"Yes."

"You knew about Eleanor."

"Yes."

"And you let it continue."

Her jaw tightened. "I told myself the work mattered more than the cost."

"And now?"

"Now the cost has names."

Nearby, a crate was being loaded onto a lorry. Files, perhaps. Or parts. Or men.

"They're issuing accident reports," she said. "For your fall. For the parachute failure. For the woman."

"She wasn't German."

"I know."

"She was right," I said. "Arthur was right. Eleanor was right."

Marwood nodded once. "That's why they're afraid."

"And London?"

"They want this to end cleanly."

"Nothing clean about it."

She allowed herself a brief, grim smile. "Clean is what they call it when the blood is dry."

A whistle blew. The camp stirred, reorganised, resumed its shape.

Hargreaves passed us without looking. Two men followed him, one carrying a case too long for papers.

"They're closing the net," Marwood said.

"Good," I replied. "They make mistakes when they hurry."

I looked back toward the marsh, toward the place where Eleanor Selwyn had stood and argued with a man who believed himself untouchable.

She had been right to be angry.

And she had been right to come here.

Daylight had explained away the night.

But it had also revealed something else.

They were no longer confident.

And that, I had learned, was when men began to break.

15

Liang Wei turned away from the wall without looking at me.

He set down his stone, wiped his hands on his trousers, and stepped away from the line as though responding to an ordinary summons. The foreman was shouting about alignment. Hammers rang. The wall rose another inch. Nothing in the rhythm changed.

I followed.

We walked along the river's edge without speaking. The water slid past the stones with its usual patience, testing each one in turn. Behind us, the wall continued its argument—slow, incremental, unpersuasive.

Liang led me to a bend where the bank dipped and the reeds grew thick, half-hidden from the camp by scrub and a shallow rise. Here the river slowed. Here the water lingered.

Here, things fell.

Liang stopped and crouched. He brushed aside dead reeds and dried silt with the back of his hand, careful not to disturb more than necessary. The motion carried the ease of repetition.

"There," he said.

I knelt beside him.

The stain was faint now. Older than yesterday. Darker where damp had held it, paler where the sun had reached. Blood loses urgency once it has had time to think.

"It washed," Liang said. "But not enough."

I nodded. The ground had done what it could. The rest had been left to us.

Liang reached into his pocket.

He did not offer what he held at once. He turned it over, weighing it, as if confirming something for himself before allowing me to see it. Then he placed it in my palm.

A pocket watch.

Silver. Scuffed. The casing dented at one edge the glass cracked but still holding. Heavier than it looked, warm from his hand.

"Found it here," Liang said. "Morning after the crash."

"You didn't give it to them."

"No."

"Why?"

"They were already explaining," he said. "This did not belong to their explanation."

I opened the case.

The face was plain. Functional. Military issue. The hands had stopped at twenty-three minutes past five. The chain was broken—snapped, not unclasped.

Inside the casing, engraved small and precise, was a name.

Sgt. A. Pike

I closed the watch.

The name settled too easily. Names do that when they arrive where they belong. It does not make them safe.

"He was here," I said.

Liang nodded once.

"When?"

"Before the fire," he said. "Before the crash."

"With her."

"Yes."

"She was angry," Liang added. "Not afraid."

Keller's words returned to me, uninvited.

"She argued," Liang went on. "Not loudly. But she did not step back."

I looked again at the stain.

"She fell here," I said.

"She was pushed," Liang replied.

That mattered.

"Who saw this?" I asked.

Liang did not answer at once. He brushed the reeds back into place, restoring the bank as much as it would allow. When he stood, his expression was carefully neutral.

"We saw enough," he said. "More than we were meant to."

"And Pike?" I asked.

Liang hesitated, then said, "He came back later."

"Alone."

"Yes."

The last uncertainty drained away.

Sergeant Pike. A British non-commissioned officer. Trusted enough to move freely. Ordinary enough to be overlooked. The sort of man who received orders quietly and carried them out without ceremony.

"Did anyone else know?" I asked.

Liang met my gaze. "Now you do."

From the camp behind us came the sound of a whistle. The labourers shifted, resumed their work. The wall continued to rise.

I slipped the watch into my pocket.

"This will cost you," I said.

Liang shrugged. "Everything costs something."

"And you?"

He looked back toward the river. "The ground remembers," he said. "Someone must listen."

When I returned to the camp, I saw Pike near the perimeter.

He leaned against a post, smoking, his cap tipped back, posture loose in the way of a man who believed himself unremarkable. He laughed at something a sentry said. He looked, in every visible way, like someone already accounted for.

The watch lay heavy in my pocket.

Not evidence yet.

Not accusation.

But no longer silence.

Pike caught my eye and nodded—casual, incurious.

I nodded back.

For the first time since I arrived on the Ness, the world did not tighten.

It steadied.

And that, I had learned, was worse.

16

Pike did not announce himself.

I knew he was there before he spoke—not from sound, exactly, but from the way the air altered, as though the land itself had made room for something it did not welcome. The shingle track along the perimeter had carried boots all day—men walking with purpose or pretending to—but this was different. This was measured. Close. Intentional.

I stopped walking.

The steps behind me did not.

"Lieutenant."

The voice came from just over my shoulder. Too close for coincidence.

I turned slowly.

Pike stood less than a yard away, positioned so that the river lay behind him and the camp behind me. It was an ordinary enough choice of ground, but I had learned to notice how men placed themselves when they meant to control outcomes rather than conversations. He had left me no easy direction to step without it being interpreted as either retreat or challenge.

His coat was unbuttoned. His cap sat too far back on his head. He looked, at first glance, like a man at ease.

I did not look at his face.

I looked at his hands.

They hung at his sides, fingers slightly curled, as though braced against cold. And they were shaking.

Not violently. It shouldn't be noticeable to casual observers. A fine tremor, irregular and persistent, passing through the fingers and gathering briefly in the knuckles before dispersing again. The sort of movement a man believes he is concealing simply by not acknowledging it.

Fear, then.

Not rage. Not heat. Fear.

"You're wandering," Pike said. "Places you don't need to be."

I said nothing. Silence, I had learned, was often more instructive than argument. It gave men space to hear themselves.

He shifted his weight. The tremor worsened for a fraction of a second, then steadied as he clenched his hands into fists and tucked them into his coat pockets. A corrective action. Learned, not instinctive.

"I'll be plain," he went on. "You've worn out your welcome."

"That suggests I was invited," I said.

He laughed—a short, brittle sound that arrived too quickly and ended too abruptly to be genuine. "You know what I mean."

"I know what you want me to understand," I replied. "That isn't always the same thing."

The wind slid across the marsh, flattening the reeds and carrying with it the faint smell of brackish water and decay.

Somewhere inland, metal struck metal—work continuing, indifferent to whatever was being settled here.

"You're causing problems," Pike said. "For people who don't like problems."

"Then they should speak to me themselves."

His jaw tightened.

"They don't need to," he said. "That's what men like me are for."

Men like me.

I let my gaze drift back, deliberately, to his hands. The tremor had not stopped. It had only been hidden.

"You followed me," I said.

He stiffened. "I am monitoring the surroundings."

"That's not what this is."

For a moment he said nothing. Then he stepped closer.

The distance between us narrowed until I could smell tobacco on his breath, stale and sweet, and something sharper beneath it—sweat, edged with anxiety rather than exertion. His voice dropped.

"You think you're clever," he said. "Listening. Watching. Putting things together."

"I think I'm doing what I was sent to do."

"No," he said. "You're doing more than that."

The words carried weight. Not a threat—not yet—but a warning sharpened by the knowledge of what followed warnings when they were ignored.

"This place runs on order," Pike continued. "On men knowing when to stop."

"And when not to?" I asked.

His eyes flicked, just once, toward the river bend—toward the reeds, the wall, the stretch of ground that had absorbed more than permitted to keep.

"She shouldn't have been there," he said.

The words fell between us and stayed there.

Something settled inside me then, the way pieces do when they finally find the shape meant to hold them.

"She knew where she was," I said.

His mouth tightened. "You don't know that."

"I know she walked the Ness like someone who had learned it," I replied. "Not like someone who wandered."

His hands came out of his pockets without his seeming to realise it. The tremor was worse now, unmistakable.

"You don't know what she was involved in," Pike said. "You don't know what she risked."

"I know what she paid."

The silence stretched. The river slid past the stones, testing the wall one inch at a time.

He leaned in until our foreheads were almost touching.

"You walk away," he said. "Today. You stop asking questions. You stop remembering things you weren't meant to see."

"And if I don't?"

His breath hitched—just once.

"Then this ends differently."

I did not move. Did not raise my voice.

"Your hands," I said.

He froze.

"What?"

"They're shaking," I said quietly. "That isn't anger. That isn't conviction. That's fear."

For a moment I thought he might strike me after all. Instead, he stepped back abruptly, as though the closeness had burned him.

"You don't understand what you're dealing with," he said.

"I understand exactly," I replied. "You were given an instruction. You carried it out. And now you're being left to carry it alone."

The tremor worsened. He clenched his fists so hard the skin went white over his knuckles.

"This is your last warning," he said.

I watched him turn away. Watched the effort it took for him to keep his hands steady as he walked.

He did not look back.

That night, I went to Shed Four.

It lay closer to the river than the others, far enough from the main cluster of buildings to be inconvenient, close enough to be explained away as necessity. The boards were older than the lock. The hinges newer than the doorframe. Someone had spent time here recently—time and effort.

I waited until the camp settled into its evening rhythms. Voices drifted. Laughter rose and fell. Engines coughed and died. Light retreated from the Ness in slow, colourless layers.

When I approached the shed, the wind was with me.

The lock resisted at first, then yielded with a soft complaint. The sound vanished almost at once, swallowed by the land.

Inside, the air was stale and metallic, tinged with oil and damp wood. No machinery stood ready. No tools lay out for honest work. The space had been emptied carefully, deliberately, leaving behind only what had been overlooked or abandoned in haste.

I moved slowly, torch hooded, letting the beam skim rather than strike.

Near the back wall, beneath a workbench pushed slightly out of true, I saw it.

A rag.

It had once been white. Now it was stiff with dried blood, darkened unevenly, as though someone had tried to wash it and failed. The fabric held its shape when I lifted it, the fibres rough beneath my fingers.

Blood that had time to soak.

Beside it lay fragments of glass.

Not debris. Not an accident.

I knelt, careful, and examined them more closely. A curved edge. A corner. The remnants of a photographic plate, shattered but not scattered, as though it had been broken quickly and left where it fell.

Images had existed here.

Then they had been corrected.

I straightened slowly. The shed seemed to draw inward around me, the river murmuring beyond the wall, patient and unpersuaded.

Pike's trembling hands returned to me—not the hands of a man consumed by rage, but of one who knew precisely what he had done and understood, too late, that obedience did not guarantee protection.

I folded the rag and replaced it exactly where I had found it. I did the same with the glass, leaving the fragments as they lay.

The ground had remembered.

Now, so had I.

17

By the afternoon, Pike had found his voice.

Not raised. Leisurely. Calm enough to pass for authority, which is always the most dangerous register. Men responded to it without quite realising they were doing so. Instructions were followed. Lines were redrawn. Small permissions vanished.

I felt it first in the way the camp moved around me.

Paths that had been open now required explanation. A sentry who had nodded yesterday now asked for my papers with a politeness that left no room for refusal. Conversations dipped when I drew near, not sharply, but with the careful timing of men who had been warned without being told why.

Containment, then.

Pike had chosen it because it was the only thing left to him that did not require courage.

I saw him again near the stores, speaking with Hargreaves. From a distance, Pike looked composed—hands folded, shoulders square, his posture that of a man who had found safety in obedience. But I had already learned the difference between control and concealment.

He did not look at me.

That mattered.

Fear that acts avoids eye contact. It does not aspire to be reminded of the moment before it committed itself.

I walked instead toward the river, letting the Ness open around me. The land was quiet in the way it always is when men attempt to impose order upon it—patient, observant, entirely unconvinced. The wall had grown again, another course of stone laid with the care of men who hoped repetition might produce permanence.

Liang Wei worked among them. He did not look up when I stopped nearby, but his voice reached me all the same.

"Someone is afraid," he said softly.

"Yes," I replied. "And afraid men make changes."

He shifted a stone into place, testing it before letting go. "Changes break things."

I followed the river eastward, away from the camp to the bend where the water slowed and darkened. The ground here had been corrected—pressed flat, reeds cut back, footprints smoothed. It had the look of a place that had been noticed too late.

I crouched and examined it properly.

The soil was firmer than it should have been. Recently compressed. A boot heel had dug in hard near the bank, the earth displaced sharply rather than worn. Another print overlapped it, angled wrong for walking.

A loss of balance.

Or a push.

The river slid past without comment. It had seen this before.

I stood as footsteps approached.

Pike stopped several paces away this time, careful to keep distance. His hands were folded again, fingers laced tight enough to whiten the skin.

"You shouldn't be here," he said.

"Neither should she have been," I replied.

He swallowed. "You were warned."

"Yes."

"And you ignored it."

"I remembered."

The wind moved through the reeds, flattening them briefly before they rose again, unchanged.

"This ends today," Pike said.

I turned to face him. His eyes were steady now, but they had the brittle quality of glass under pressure.

"What ends?" I asked.

"This uncertainty," he said. "Rumours. Men talking. Accidents beginning to look deliberate."

"And are they?" I asked.

His jaw tightened. "That depends on who's looking."

A shout carried from the camp. Urgent. Uncontrolled.

Pike turned instinctively, and in that moment the mask slipped. Fear, stripped of preparation, flashed across his face.

A corporal ran toward us, breathless. "Sergeant—there's been a problem."

Pike did not take his eyes off me. "Speak."

"The photography hut," the man said. "Someone's been inside. Plates are missing."

Missing, not broken.

Pike closed his eyes briefly.

That was when I knew he had already lost control.

He moved quickly then, too quickly, and I followed at a distance. The hut stood open, the canvas flap lifting weakly in the wind like a failed signal. Inside, the air was thick with chemicals and something sharper—panic, unresolved.

A young technician stood by the racks, pale and shaking. Hollis hovered near the back wall, his ink-stained fingers clenched uselessly at his sides.

"How many?" Pike asked.

"Three. Maybe four," the technician said. "From the marsh run. High-angle."

From before the crash.

Pike's shoulders sagged, just enough to notice.

"Who logged them out?" he asked.

The technician hesitated.

Pike stepped closer. "Who."

"Hollis did," the man blurted.

Hollis looked up sharply. "I—"

"Enough," Pike snapped.

I watched Hollis then, the way his face folded inward as the weight settled. Not guilt. Recognition. He understood suddenly where he stood in the structure Pike was building.

Pike turned to me. "You did this."

"I wasn't here," I said. "And neither were you."

His hands twitched.

"You think this makes you clever," he said. "Forcing movement."

"I think it makes you careless," I replied. "And carelessness leaves witnesses."

"Witnesses can be persuaded," Pike said.

"Not the land," I said. "Not men who have already seen too much."

Hollis spoke then, quietly. "The plate from Shed Four," he said.

Pike spun on him. "What about it?"

"It wasn't just broken," Hollis said. "Someone smashed it, yes—but they left the emulsion intact. Like they didn't want it destroyed. Just ... unusable."

Correction.

Pike stared at him as if seeing him for the first time. Not as an accomplice, but as a liability.

"You're done here," Pike said. "Pack your things."

Hollis blinked. "Sir?"

"Now."

Hollis did not move.

"If he goes," I said, "someone will ask why."

Pike rounded on me. "You've done enough."

"Not yet," I replied. "But you have."

The river moved past the hut, patient and indifferent.

Pike looked at me then—really looked—and something passed between us. Not agreement. Recognition.

"You won't stop," he said.

"No," I said. "And neither will the ground."

He exhaled slowly.

That was the moment fear slipped fully into consequence.

18

Fear does not rush.

That was the mistake I had made at first—assuming Pike's fear would drive him to something crude, something visible. It did not. It refined him. It taught him to manoeuvre, to act in increments small enough to pass as procedure.

By the next morning, the camp had been reorganised.

Not overtly. Nothing that could be pointed to and named as a restriction. But the paths I had taken freely the day before now required explanation. A sentry who had once waved me through now checked my papers with apologetic thoroughness. A door that had been unlocked yesterday was closed today—not barred, simply ... decided.

Containment had ceased to be a word.

It had become a behaviour.

I saw Pike near the stores shortly after dawn. He was speaking with Hargreaves, his posture attentive, his tone respectful. From a distance, he looked like a man who had found his footing again. His hands were still. His voice carried. His authority had gained substance.

He did not look at me.

That mattered.

Men who intend violence watch you. Men who intend procedure avoid you. They do not want to be reminded that what they are about to do will have a face.

I did not approach him.

Instead, I walked the perimeter.

The Ness lay pale and flat beneath a sky scrubbed nearly colourless. The river slid along its uncertain course, testing the stones of the wall with the patience of something that knew it would outlast any argument raised against it. The labourers were already at work, shoulders bent, movements careful. Liang Wei did not look up as I passed, but the man beside him did—just long enough to register my presence before returning to his task.

Someone had spoken to them.

Not to silence them. Not yet.

To measure them.

That was Pike's doing.

I followed the river eastward, toward the bend where the ground still remembered more than it was supposed to. The reeds there had been cut back again. The bank smoothed. The scuffed earth pressed flat beneath boots that had stood too long in one place.

Correction, again.

I crouched and pressed my palm to the soil. It was cold and firm the damp driven down by repeated weight. This was not erosion. This was editing.

When I stood, Hollis was there.

He had not approached loudly. He had not called my name. Standing a few steps back, with his hands clasped in front, his ink-stained fingers scrubbed until they were raw.

"You shouldn't be here," he said.

"Neither should you," I replied.

His mouth twitched—not quite a smile. "They've started asking questions."

"Who?"

He hesitated. "People who already know the answers."

London, then.

"Pike?" I asked.

Hollis nodded once. "He's been instructed."

That was new.

"By whom?"

Hollis looked past me, toward the river. "That's above my grade."

We stood in silence for a moment, the wind flattening the reeds and lifting them again, unchanged.

"They know about the plates," he said.

"I assumed as much."

"They know they're missing," he went on. "They know what they show. Or at least what they suggest."

"And they know you handled them."

His shoulders tightened. "Yes."

"Are you being blamed?"

"Not yet," he said. "I'm being ... evaluated."

I studied him more closely then. Hollis had always been careful, always half a step back from the work itself, recording rather than shaping. He was not a man built for confrontation. But something had shifted in him. His fear had not turned inward.

It had spun.

"What did you see?" I asked.

He swallowed. "Enough."

"That's not an answer."

"It's the only one I can give," he said. Then, after a pause, "They don't want me gone. They want me compliant."

"And Pike?"

"He wants me quiet."

"Those are not the same thing."

"No," Hollis agreed. "They rarely are."

We parted without ceremony. That, too, felt deliberate.

By midday, the pressure became explicit.

A civilian lorry arrived without markings. No insignia. No explanation. Two men stepped out, coats too well cut for the weather, expressions composed into neutrality. They did not look around the camp with curiosity. They looked around it with ownership.

London had arrived.

Not officially. It's not something that would need to be documented. But the effect was immediate.

Hargreaves became smaller.

Pike became busier.

I was summoned to the communications hut just after noon.

The message was brief. Typed. Unadorned.

Return to London at once. Your presence at Orford Ness is no longer required.

Unsigned.

Authority does not need a name when it is confident.

I wrote my reply beneath it in pencil.

Investigation incomplete. Evidence discovered. Will report in person.

The operator's eyes flicked up, then away. He did not comment.

Outside, Pike was waiting.

He stood alone this time, near the edge of the camp where the Ness opened wide and indifferent. His hands were folded behind his back his posture faultless.

"They are expecting you to leave," he remarked.

"They want silence," I replied.

He did not argue.

"You're finished here," he went on. "This has gone far enough."

"For whom?"

"For everyone," he said. "Including you."

I watched his face as he spoke. The fear was still there, but it had been organised now, channelled into obedience. Pike had chosen his side.

"Arthur Selwyn," I said.

The name landed.

Pike did not flinch, but the skin around his eyes tightened.

"That's not relevant," he said.

"It's the only thing that is."

"You don't know what you're playing with," he said.

"I know exactly," I replied. "You've been told to make this disappear. And you've mistaken removal for resolution."

His voice dropped. "You leave today."

"And if I don't?"

His jaw worked. "Then this stops being administrative."

That night, someone slid a note under my door.

I heard it before I saw it—the faint whisper of paper against wood, the subtle displacement of air. I waited until the footsteps retreated before opening the door.

The corridor was empty.

The note lay on the floor, folded once. No name. No seal. Just four words, written in block capitals.

THE NESS REMEMBERS.

I held it for a long moment, the paper warming in my hand.

A warning.

Or a threat.

Someone wanted me to know I was being watched. Or that I was not alone. Possibly both.

I thought of Liang Wei. Of Hollis. Of the technician who had gone pale when the plates vanished. Of Pike, standing straighter now, fear hardened into procedure.

And of Eleanor Selwyn, who had walked this land knowing exactly what it remembered.

I folded the note and slipped it into my pocket.

The ground remembers.

The question now was who was listening—and who was afraid enough to act.

17

Hargreaves chose the office.

That alone told me this would not be denial.

He could have met me outside, where rank and distance do the work. Summoning guards, paperwork, or London were all within his power. Instead, he closed the door himself and drew the blinds with unnecessary care.

Daylight filtered in regardless.

"You wanted to speak to me," he said.

"I wanted you to stop lying," I said.

He did not bristle. He did not bluster. He sat slowly, as if the chair had always been waiting for him. For a moment he looked older than before, the lines at the edges of his eyes no longer performing authority.

"You're past accusations," he said. "So am I."

"That depends on what you admit."

He folded his hands on the desk.

"I knew her," he said.

Not *the woman*.

Not *the victim*.

Her.

The admission landed without force. It did not need any.

"What did you know her as?" I asked.

He hesitated.

"Evelyn," he said. "That's what she called herself."

The name sat badly against everything else I knew. Which meant it was probably true.

"And Eleanor Selwyn?"

His eyes closed briefly.

"Yes," he said. "That too."

I did not interrupt.

"She came to me first," Hargreaves went on. "Not officially. She knew better. She said she was asking questions no one wanted answered."

"She wasn't wrong."

"No," he said. "She wasn't."

"You didn't report her."

"No."

"Why?"

He smiled faintly, without humour. "Because I told myself she was already frightened enough."

That caught.

"Frightened of what?"

"Of Dr Marwood," he said.

The name entered the room like a pressure change.

"She believed Marwood had crossed a line," Hargreaves continued. "Not out of malice. Out of compliance. She said Marwood believed the work mattered more than the cost."

"And did it?"

"That's the trap, Lieutenant," he said. "Once you measure cost, you're already complicit."

"You didn't kill her."

"No."

"And you didn't order it."

"No."

"But you knew she was in danger."

"Yes."

"And you did nothing."

"Yes."

That, I understood, was the confession he had come prepared to give.

"Why tell me now?"

He looked up.

"Because you're already below the surface," he said. "And because what's underneath doesn't care who survives the telling."

He stood and crossed to the back of the hut. He lifted a section of floor matting I had assumed was there to keep the damp down.

It wasn't.

Beneath it lay a metal hatch, its outline disguised with deliberate care. The bolts were new. The metal was too clean.

"You won't find this on any map," Hargreaves said. "Or in any ledger you're meant to see."

"You're showing me, anyway."

"Yes."

"Why?"

"Since it will be found anyway," he remarked. "And I'd rather not be remembered as the man who tried to stop you."

He turned the handle.

The hatch opened downward, releasing a breath of air that smelled wrong—oil, iron, something faintly electrical.

A tunnel.

Not brick. Not stone. Reinforced concrete, poured in sections, the seams disguised with paint and shadow. A cable ran along one wall, pulsing faintly.

Alive!

Beneath the airfield.

"How long has this been here?" I asked.

"Longer than the Zeppelin," he said. "Shorter than the war."

We descended.

The sound reached us halfway down—not loud, but constant.

A hum.

Machinery under load. Not idle. Not testing.

Working.

At the base of the ladder, the tunnel widened into a passage tall enough to walk without stooping. The walls bore marks of hurried construction: chalk numbers, half-painted arrows, measurements scratched out and redrawn.

Containment poured into concrete.

We stopped at a sealed door.

Steel. Riveted. Newer than everything around it. The hum was louder here, resonant, like breath forced through metal lungs.

"What's behind it?" I asked.

Hargreaves did not answer at once.

"Proof," he said finally. "Or damnation. The difference is mostly paperwork."

"And Eleanor?"

"She found this," he said. "Or enough of it. Enough to understand Arthur hadn't vanished. He'd been absorbed."

"And when she threatened exposure?"

"She became a variable," Hargreaves said quietly. "Variables get corrected."

I thought of Pike's trembling hands.

Of the broken plates.

Of blood that had not washed away.

"She argued with Pike."

Hargreaves nodded. "His purpose was to intimidate her."

"But fear is unreliable."

"Yes."

I stepped closer to the door.

"Do you hear that?" I asked.

The hum deepened, as if answering.

"Whatever this is," I said, "it's not meant to stay hidden."

"No," Hargreaves said. "It's meant to finish."

I reached for the handle.

Behind me, Hargreaves spoke once more.

"If you open that door," he said, "there's no returning to observation."

"I know."

I pulled.

The seal broke with a sound like breath escaping a lung.

The machinery beyond surged, louder now, undeniable.

Containment had failed again.

This time underground.

And whatever had been built to remain unseen was about to be forced into daylight.

18

The storm arrived without warning.

Not as thunder or spectacle, but as pressure—air thickening, light flattening, the sky lowering until it felt less like weather and more like weight. By the time Hargreaves and I stood before the sealed door beneath the airfield, rain was already needling the ground above us, finding weaknesses the way truth does.

The hum never stopped.

It filled the tunnel with vibration you felt in the teeth before you heard it properly, a sound that had been running too long to remember what silence was. Whatever lay behind the door did not sleep.

Hargreaves stood a step back now. He had brought me this far, and no further.

"Once it's open," he said, "there's no language for what follows."

"There never is," I said.

I turned the handle.

The resistance was brief—the kind designed to satisfy procedure rather than prevent action. The seal broke with a hiss like breath escaping a lung. Warm air pushed out, smelling of oil, ozone, damp metal—and something else beneath it, faint but unmistakable.

Decay.

The door swung inward.

The chamber beyond was larger than the tunnel suggested. Long rather than wide, its ceiling braced with steel ribs that disappeared into shadow. Lamps hung at intervals, some lit, others dark, creating pools of light broken by long bands of gloom. Cables ran along the walls like veins, disappearing through ducts and grates, feeding whatever machinery laboured deeper inside.

At first, it looked like an engine room.

Then the shapes resolved.

Tables. Cradles. Rigs bolted directly into the floor. Not built for comfort. Built for repetition. Built to be hosed down.

The hum grew louder as we stepped inside—not from volume, but proximity. It pressed against the eardrums, turned thought into effort.

"This isn't naval," I said.

"No," Hargreaves replied. "It's adjacent."

That was his gift: a vocabulary that made monstrosities administrative.

Rainwater was already seeping down the tunnel behind us, carrying grit and leaves and the smell of the Ness into the chamber. The storm overhead was discovering weaknesses in the structure quicker than the builders ever expected.

Containment was failing on every level.

We moved deeper.

I saw the scorch marks first—irregular patterns on the floor, blackened and smeared as though something had resisted burning. Nearby, a steel frame lay twisted, one joint fused by heat, another snapped clean. Instruments had been smashed and then partially replaced, the way one repairs a lie rather than corrects it.

A failed experiment.

Not abandoned. Interrupted.

The walls bore chalk markings: figures, symbols, shorthand only engineers would read without hesitation. Some had been scrubbed away and rewritten. Others crossed out entirely. Trial numbers repeated with slight variation, as though persistence alone might turn error into success.

Hargreaves did not look at them.

He watched me instead.

"You understand what this meant to do," he said.

"I understand it was never meant to be seen," I said.

He nodded. That was close enough to an agreement.

The body lay at the far end of the chamber.

Not hidden. Not ceremonially arranged. Simply left where it had fallen, as though death itself had been deemed sufficient explanation.

Arthur Selwyn.

He was smaller than I had imagined. Or perhaps death had reduced him, drawn him inward. His clothes were those of a working engineer—practical, worn—but stiff now, fused to him in places by heat and fluid. One arm lay at an angle that suggested it had been broken before he stopped moving.

There was no attempt to make him disappear.

Only to make him irrelevant.

I knelt beside him.

The floor here was scored with deep gouges, as though something heavy had been dragged away. A blood smear led from his side toward a drain cut into the concrete. The drain was clogged now, choked with debris the storm had pushed back up from the river.

Even the building itself resisted.

"He didn't die instantly," I said.

Hargreaves did not answer.

I touched Arthur's sleeve. The fabric crumbled slightly beneath my fingers, ash-dry in places. Whatever they had tested here involved heat—controlled, they would have said. Calculated.

Containment.

I stood.

Along the wall beside Arthur was a clipboard, still hanging from a hook. The paper clipped to it had yellowed but remained legible.

A list.

Names, typed. Columns neatly ruled. Beside each name, a designation.

Some crossed through. Some circled. Some marked with a single word, written in Marwood's hand.

Containment

Arthur Selwyn's name sat at the top.

Below it were others.

Engineers. Technicians. A medical orderly.

And halfway down the page:

Evelyn

Not Eleanor.

Evelyn.

No surname.

The name she used with Hargreaves. The name she carried when she walked the Ness. The name she spoke when she argued by the river.

Marked for containment.

My mouth went dry.

"She was never meant to leave," I said.

Hargreaves's voice was quiet behind me. "Her fear should have kept her quiet."

"And when she wasn't?"

He did not answer.

The storm chose that moment to announce itself properly.

Thunder rolled across the Ness—not sharp, but sustained, as though the sky itself were tearing fabric. The lights in the chamber flickered once, twice, then steadied again.

For now.

Water seeped through the ceiling joints, dripping onto machinery in irregular patterns. Sparks leapt where droplets struck exposed contacts. Somewhere above us, men were shouting orders.

The river wall.

I felt it then—pressure pushing back through places it had been forced away from. The wall Liang and the others were building was arguing with the storm, and the storm was winning.

The Ness remembers.

And it collects its debts.

The hum changed pitch.

Lower. Strained.

"Power's fluctuating," Hargreaves said.

"That's not power," I said. "That's panic."

I moved further into the chamber.

Beyond Arthur's body was the core of the experiment. A cylindrical housing split along one seam, its interior blackened. Inside lay fragments of something that had once been uniform—metal plates warped, fastenings melted, insulation burned through.

An explosion, then containment.

A failure they could not explain without implicating themselves.

Arthur Selwyn had been in the way.

"Was he alone?" I asked.

"Yes."

"That's a lie."

Hargreaves closed his eyes briefly. "He wasn't meant to be."

"Who was?"

He opened them. "Marwood."

That name again.

"She designed the protocols," he said. "The safety margins. The revisions."

"And the list."

"Yes."

The storm struck harder now, rain hammering into the tunnel mouth, water beginning to run along the floor in shallow streams. The drain near Arthur overflowed, releasing a smell that turned my stomach.

Decay does not stay buried when water is involved.

I took the ledger from my coat.

Marwood's book.

I held it beneath the lamp and flipped to the pages I had marked. The same names appeared there, reduced to initials, then to letters, then to numbers.

Containment was not a response.

It was a process.

"You were cleaning up," I said. "One variable at a time."

"Yes," Hargreaves said. "And then Eleanor saw the pattern."

"She wasn't on the list at first."

"No."

"But she put herself there."

He nodded.

"She learned too much."

I thought of the photograph—Evelyn standing with Hollis and Pritchard, coat open, silk visible, refusing to step back.

Of Pike's trembling hands.

The lights flickered again, longer this time. The hum stuttered, then resumed at a harsher pitch.

Something deep in the machinery gave a metallic groan.

"This place isn't built to flood," I said.

"No," Hargreaves said. "It was built to be forgotten."

Another roll of thunder. The sound echoed down the tunnel, amplified, distorted, until it sounded like movement rather than weather.

I tore the list from the clipboard.

Hargreaves watched me do it.

"London will deny this exists," he said.

"Of course they will."

"They'll call it enemy sabotage. A German device. An unfortunate accident."

"Containment."

"Yes."

I folded the list into the ledger.

The chamber lights went out.

For a moment there was nothing but the hum and the sound of water rushing where it did not belong.

Then the emergency lamps flared, casting everything in a sickly amber glow.

Arthur Selwyn's face looked different in that light—less like a corpse, more like a witness.

The floor shuddered.

Somewhere above us, the river wall failed.

Not all at once. Not catastrophically. Just enough.

Water surged down the tunnel in a sudden wave, cold and fast, sweeping debris with it. I staggered and caught myself against the wall. Hargreaves slipped, went down hard, his shout lost in the roar.

The hum cut out.

Silence hit like a blow.

Shortly thereafter, alarms sounded—subdued and remote, as if their activation were tentative or subject to approval.

"We need to go," Hargreaves said, hauling himself upright.

I looked once more at Arthur Selwyn.

"I'm not leaving him," I said.

"You can't take him," Hargreaves replied. "Not like this."

"No," I said. "But I can take his story."

Another surge rushed past us, higher now, carrying tools, paper, fragments of chalk-marked boards. The chamber was becoming a river.

I turned and ran.

The tunnel behind us was half-flooded already, water climbing the ladder rungs. The storm had found every shortcut the builders had ignored.

We climbed.

By the time we emerged into the hut above, soaked and gasping, the airfield was chaos—men shouting, lights swinging, ground softening as water forced its way up from below.

The Ness reclaiming.

Hargreaves leaned against the wall, breathing hard.

"It won't stay hidden now," he said.

"No," I replied. "It never was."

Sirens wailed in the distance—real ones now, not administrative approximations. Someone had finally decided this was worth noticing.

I looked back at the hatch.

Water spilled from it, carrying the smell of oil and death and secrets that had never learned how to remain buried.

Arthur Selwyn had not vanished.

Evelyn had not imagined it.

Containment had failed.

And there would be no repairing what the storm had revealed.

The ground remembers.

And now, so did everyone else.

19

The storm did not end when we climbed out of the hatch. It merely changed its tactics.

Above ground the rain came sideways now, driven hard enough to sting, needling through seams in canvas and collars and the thin pretence of authority. Water ran in shallow sheets across the airfield, turning shingle to slurry, forcing men to place each step with care, as though the ground itself could no longer be trusted.

Which, I realised, it could not.

The Ness answered.

Hargreaves leaned against the hut wall, breathing hard, one hand pressed to his side as though holding himself together by habit alone. His uniform, once immaculate, clung damply to him now. His face showed no sign of fear.

It was a calculation that had exhausted its numbers.

Behind us, the hatch continued to disgorge water, as though the earth had taken a mouthful and spat. It carried the smell with it—oil, rust, ozone, and something older.

Something that had been kept too long in the dark.

Men ran toward us, then slowed when they saw Hargreaves. They did not ask questions. They did not look at the water. They looked at *him*, waiting for their reality to be assigned.

Hargreaves straightened, remembering his shape.

"Back," he snapped. "Back to your stations."

There were no stations now. Not really. There was only motion.

A lorry skidded as it turned, tyres carving grooves into the soaked ground. Someone shouted "generator" and then shouted it again, louder, as though volume alone might repair machinery. A flare went up—white against grey—then vanished into the rain like a thought dismissed.

Containment, I thought.

Not a word.

A reflex.

I kept my hand on the ledger beneath my coat, feeling the press of paper and the folded list inside it. My other hand brushed the scrap of silk, still there, still warm. Evidence now. Not symbolic. Not theoretical.

Hargreaves followed my glance.

"You've got what you came for," he said. "Now you go."

"Where?" I asked.

He looked at me as if the question were childish. "Away. London. Anywhere that isn't here."

"And you?" I asked.

His mouth tightened. "I manage what can still be managed."

"By calling it something else," I said.

His eyes flickered. "Choose your language carefully."

"I have," I said. "That's why I'm still standing."

The sirens rose again—real ones this time, not the polite approximations the camp preferred. Their pitch climbed and held, insistent, as though the world had finally decided to acknowledge what it had been told to ignore.

Men began to look at one another now, not at Hargreaves.

That shift mattered.

Authority works best when it goes unquestioned. Chaos asks questions simply by existing.

Hargreaves pushed away from the wall.

"I never wanted you below," he said.

"I know," I replied. "You brought me anyway."

He stared at me for a long moment, resentment, and something like relief crossing his face.

"Because you were going to find it," he said. "And if you'd found it alone, you'd have done something stupid."

"What would have been stupid?" I asked.

He smiled thinly. "Thinking the truth is enough."

A gust struck the hut, shaking the canvas. Water ran down the seams in sudden rivulets. Somewhere nearby a man slipped and went down hard, swore once, then swallowed the sound as though afraid of being overheard even by the weather.

The Ness was teaching everyone the same lesson.

Control fails.

Only the timing differs.

I moved away from the hatch. The men parted without meaning to, as though my coat carried something they did not want close.

I had taken only paper.

But paper, I had learned, outweighed bodies.

I was nearly clear of the airfield when a voice spoke my name.

Not shouted.

Not urgent.

Placed with care.

"Lieutenant Quirk."

I turned.

Dr. Elspeth Marwood stood beneath the eaves of a hangar, sheltered from the worst of the rain. Her cap was straight. Her hair pinned neatly. She looked as though this were an interruption rather than a crisis.

That frightened me more than the storm.

Behind her, men moved crates—files, instruments, long metal cases—working quickly and without comment. The work of relocation, not repair.

"You shouldn't be here," she said.

"I could say the same," I replied.

She stepped closer. The rain beaded on her coat without seeming to touch her composure.

"You went down," she said.

"Yes."

"And you opened it."

"Yes."

Her eyes flicked once—to my coat.

"You took something."

"I preserved what was there," I said.

"That's an indulgent way to describe theft," she replied.

"It's a precise one," I said.

For a moment she said nothing. Sirens rose and fell behind us. A generator drowned somewhere to our left.

"Do you know what you've done?" she asked.

"I've seen what you were hiding," I said. "What happens to those who see it?"

Her expression tightened, not in denial but in correction.

"'Hiding' implies shame," she said. "This wasn't shame."

"It was secrecy," I said.

"Secrecy is not always a sin," she replied. "Sometimes it's the only thing that keeps a nation intact."

She believed this.

Not as an excuse.

A doctrine.

"You call it containment," I said.

"Yes."

"And you write it over names," I said. "Like a verdict."

"Like a function," she corrected. "A procedure."

"A euphemism," I said.

"You're sentimental," she replied.

"I'm observant."

She lowered her voice.

"You saw the chamber. You saw the necessity of it."

"I saw Arthur Selwyn," I said.

Her gaze did not flinch.

"An unfortunate outcome," she said.

"An outcome," I echoed.

"You think war is clean?" she asked. "Results manifest regardless of whether they are explicitly identified."

"You left him there."

"He could not be moved," she said. "And he could not be spoken of."

"That's containment," I said. "Removal."

"You confuse containment with murder," she said.

"I don't," I replied. "The list marked Evelyn."

A pause.

"You saw the list."

"Yes."

"And you understand why it exists."

"I understand you were prepared to erase her."

"She forced our hand."

"She forced your conscience."

Marwood looked past me toward the spreading water.

"Conscience is a peacetime luxury," she said.

"And truth?" I asked.

She turned back, calm sharpening.

"Truth is whatever does the least harm."

"And who decides to harm?"

She did not smile.

"Men in rooms you were summoned to," she said.

She stepped closer.

"Stop digging."

The words were simple. Final.

"Or what?" I asked.

Her gaze drifted to my shoulder, my pocket, the parts of me that could be broken and explained.

"You've seen how accidents are made," she said.

The parachute.

The plate.

The fuel line.

The shove in the dark.

"They'll blame Keller," she said.

The name struck hard.

"And Pike?" I asked.

Another pause.

"Pike was useful," she said. "Now he's unstable."

"You're eliminating everyone who knows," I said.

"We are limiting exposure."

"It's the same thing."

"It isn't," she said. "One is cruelty. The other is survival."

She stepped back, granting me space as proof of reasonableness.

"This is your last warning," she said. "Leave with your life intact."

"And if I don't?"

"You'll be corrected," she said. "Like the rest."

She turned away.

Behind her, London moved quietly. Doors locked. Crates vanished. Accidents were already being written.

I stood in the rain the ledger pressed against my ribs like a second heart.

Marwood believed memory could be contained.

She was mistaken.

So was anyone who thought I would stop now.

Because I finally understood what I was facing.

Not a killer.

A system.

And systems do not rage.

They are correct.

20

By morning, the story had settled.

Not into truth, but into something usable.

I understood this before anyone spoke to me, from the way the camp arranged itself around my presence. Paths I had walked freely the day before now required explanation. Doors remained open but were suddenly watched. Conversations thinned as I approached, not stopping outright—just losing weight, as though my proximity altered what could safely be said.

I was no longer an investigator.

I was an interruption.

The accusation arrived wrapped in procedure.

Two officers I did not recognise were waiting outside the communications hut when I was intercepted. They wore identical expressions—polite, incurious, already resolved.

"Lieutenant Quirk," one of them said. "You're required to accompany us."

"On what grounds?" I asked.

He consulted the paper in his hand, though I suspected he could have recited it from memory.

"Interference with military operations," he said. "Unauthorised access to restricted areas. Failure to comply with recall instructions."

He looked up then, just long enough to deliver the final clause.

"Conduct inconsistent with the requirements of wartime discipline."

There it was.

Not murder.

Not obstruction of justice.

Discipline.

"I object," I said.

"Noted," he replied, and gestured for me to walk.

They did not touch me. That mattered. Physical restraint would have made this something else—something louder. This appeared cooperative.

We passed through the camp in daylight, and I felt the shift take hold fully then. Men who had nodded to me before now looked past. A few looked too long, curiosity already being repackaged as suspicion.

Unstable.

Over-involved.

Not quite reliable.

The door they led me through was not a cell.

It was a storeroom.

Bare boards. A table. Two chairs. A small window placed too high to be useful. A guard was positioned outside, observable through the open doorway, engaged in reading a document that appeared unnecessary for his duties.

"You're not under arrest," the officer said. "This is a temporary holding measure."

"Until when?"

"Until the War Office decides what to do with you."

That could mean anything. Which was the point?

They left me there with my coat, my hat, and nothing else. The ledger had been removed without comment. That, too, was deliberate.

Paper first.

Men later.

The dynamics of time undergo significant alteration when it is employed as a strategic asset.

I do not know how long I sat there. Long enough for the sounds of the camp to resume their rhythm without me. Long enough for the silence to feel intentional. Long enough to understand that this was not about researching.

It was about shaping a narrative.

The War Office arrived by wire.

Not directly, of course. That would imply engagement. Instead, a major I had never met came in, carrying a folder that already had my name on it.

"You've put us in a difficult position," he said, sitting without invitation.

"I wasn't aware your position was fragile," I replied.

He smiled thinly. "This is exactly the type of comment that gives us cause for concern."

He opened the folder.

He continued by stating, "You have exhibited a consistent pattern of behaviour. Persistent. Obstructive. Resistant to instruction. Under normal circumstances, one might admire that."

"And under wartime ones?"

"Under wartime ones," he said, "it becomes dangerous."

He spoke of morale. Of the need for unity. Of how easily rumours spread among men already strained beyond reason. He spoke carefully, choosing phrases that did not accuse but implied.

"You've pursued personal theories," he said. "Ignored proper channels. Involved civilians. Foreign nationals."

"Keller," I said.

"Yes," he replied smoothly. "The German airman. A highly unreliable witness."

"He told the truth," I said.

The major closed the folder.

"That is not for you to decide," he said. "Your role is to observe, report, and withdraw when instructed. You have done only the first of these."

"And the truth?" I asked.

"The truth," he said, "is what allows the war to continue."

That was as close as he came to honesty.

He stood.

"You will return to London," he said. "Immediately. The case at Orford Ness is closed."

"And if I refuse?"

He looked at me for a moment, considering.

"Then we will have to reassess your fitness for continued service," he said. "Exhaustion can manifest in... fixation. You've been through a great deal."

There it was again.

Not wrong.

Unwell.

I was left alone once more.

That was when Keller came.

I did not hear him at first. Only the guard shifting outside, the sound of a chair scraping softly. Then Keller was standing in the doorway, escorted by a corporal who looked profoundly uncomfortable.

The corporal did not meet my eyes.

"You have five minutes," he said. "Then he's transferred."

Keller stepped inside and closed the door behind him.

"They are going to blame me," he said without preamble.

"Yes," I replied. "They are."

He nodded, as if confirming something he had already accepted.

"But you are still here," he said. "That means they are not finished."

"Not with you," I said. "And not with me."

Keller looked at the window, at the light that refused to be useful.

"I saw her argue with him," he said quietly. "By the river. I said this already."

"I know."

"They told me I was confused," he said. "They said the crash had made me imagine things."

I said nothing.

Keller leaned closer.

"There is a way out," he said. "Not officially."

I looked at him then.

"You're being transferred," I said. "You don't have leverage."

He shook his head. "I have invisibility," he said. "It is very powerful."

He explained quickly. The supply track behind the sheds. A gate left unlatched during the storm. A lorry scheduled to leave within the hour, carrying equipment no one wanted to catalogue too closely.

"They will not look for you immediately," Keller said. "They will be too busy explaining why you were detained in the first place."

"And you?" I asked.

He smiled, small and tired.

"They are already blaming me," he said. "If I help you, nothing changes. If I do not, I will always know what I failed to do."

The choice, then, was not really mine.

The corporal returned. Keller stepped back, already resuming the posture of a prisoner.

As he passed me, he spoke without turning his head.

"Walk when the engine starts," he said. "Do not run."

They took him away.

I waited.

When the lorry's engine coughed into life, I stood.

No one stopped me.

That was the strangest part of all.

I walked through the gate Keller had described my pace steady, my expression neutral. The driver did not look at me. He did not need to. He had been instructed not to.

Behind me, the camp continued to close ranks. Paperwork would follow. Explanations would be drafted. My absence would be described as unfortunate, perhaps regrettable, but ultimately inconsequential.

They would say I interfered.

They would say I lost objectivity.

They would say I became unstable.

And somewhere in Whitehall, someone would decide whether my story was worth correcting.

I did not look back.

The Ness does not reward that.

As the road carried me away from the airfield, I understood something with a clarity that settled deep and cold.

The walls had closed in.

But they had closed too late.

Because the truth was no longer contained in one place.

And because Keller—dismissed, foreign, expendable—had chosen to open a door they had forgotten to guard.

The war would go on.

But so would memory.

And now, so would I.

21

The camera was not supposed to see that far.

That was the first thing Arthur Selwyn understood, and the last thing he said out loud.

I learned this not from confession or memorandum, but from the quiet, embarrassed way the engineers spoke about the apparatus once they realised I already knew too much. The RFC's experimental division had been testing a new aerial camera—long-range, high-altitude, capable of resolving detail from heights that made even seasoned pilots uneasy. The surrounding language was careful, technical, reverent. Precision optics. Improved plates. A step ahead of the enemy.

The issue did not lie in the camera's intended purpose or its visual capabilities.

The problem was what it saw anyway.

At altitude, the Earth simplifies. Features flatten. Patterns emerge. Camouflage relies on confusion of scale, on the assumption that no one will ever look from quite that angle, at quite that distance, with quite that clarity.

Arthur Selwyn had looked.

The camera had gone up during a routine test flight—no enemy contact, no deviation from plan. The pilot had followed his course the plates had been exposed, and the aircraft had returned with nothing more remarkable than icy fingers and a complaint about the wind shear.

The discovery came later in the darkroom.

A shadow where there should not have been one. A geometry that did not belong to marsh or shingle or sea. Straight lines intersecting at angles too deliberate for erosion. A scar in the coastline that refused every explanation offered for it.

A restricted naval installation.

Not on any map Arthur Selwyn had clearance to see. Not marked, not named, not acknowledged. Dry docks disguised as tidal pools. Slipways masked as natural inlets. Structures built to be mistaken for absence.

The camera had not known what it was photographing.

Arthur had.

He had traced the lines with his finger while the plate was still wet, his breath held as though the image might shift if disturbed. He had checked the flight path. The altitude. The exposure time. He had told himself it was an error.

Then he had checked again.

Arthur Selwyn was not reckless. He did not storm offices or raise his voice. He did what engineers do when confronted with impossibility: he verified.

And once verification failed to make the problem go away, he spoke.

That was his mistake.

By the time I understood this fully, the storm had returned.

Not abruptly. Not theatrically. It gathered instead, as it had before—pressure building, light draining of warmth, the air thickening until movement itself felt provisional. The Ness darkened under it, the river rising against the wall with renewed insistence.

I stood at the edge of the airfield as the first rain struck, watching the clouds settle into position like an argument that had been rehearsed.

The sheds were quieter now.

Too quiet.

Where there had been movement—men, equipment, the small industry of experimentation—there was only absence. Doors stood open where they had been locked the day before. Others were sealed without explanation. The photography hut was dark, its windows covered, its contents removed.

Marwood had vanished.

Not dramatically. No escort. No farewell. She had simply ceased to be present, as though the camp had exhaled her.

That, more than anything else, told me the truth had reached its next phase.

Containment did not always require elimination.

Sometimes it required relocation.

As the rain started coming down heavily, I made my way back to the river wall. The labourers had been sent away, their tools stacked neatly, their work paused mid-argument. The water pressed against the stones, testing each one as patiently as ever.

Arthur Selwyn had done the same.

He had taken the plates to his immediate superior first, not as an accusation but as an inquiry. Could this be right? Could this installation be ours? The response had been swift and strangely bloodless. The images were confiscated. Arthur was thanked for his diligence. He was told gently that the matter would be handled at a higher level.

He did not accept that.

He made copies.

That was the second mistake.

The third assumption stated that notifying about a breach would lead to the issue being escalated to senior management. Arthur had believed in process. He had believed that the system corrected itself when properly informed.

What he had not understood was that the system had already seen what he saw.

It had simply decided not to acknowledge it.

The storm thickened, the rain flattening the reeds and lifting them again, unchanged. Somewhere inland, a generator coughed and fell silent. The camp lights flickered once, then steadied, drawing power from reserves meant for emergencies rather than truth.

I strolled the perimeter, my pace unhurried, my posture deliberately unremarkable. When pressure is highest, appearing guilty may be riskier than actually being guilty.

I did not hurry.

Arthur Selwyn had hurried.

Once the copies existed, the decision was no longer theoretical. Reporting the breach meant admitting that a camera designed to out-see the enemy had seen too much of ourselves. It meant acknowledging a vulnerability that could not be explained without unravelling months—years—of secrecy.

Arthur had threatened to report it anyway.

Not to the camp.

To Whitehall.

That was the moment containment began.

The storm rolled fully in then, rain hammering the airfield hard enough to blur edges and flatten sound. Water ran where it pleased, refusing drains, ignoring channels. The Ness has always been better at reclaiming than surrendering.

I took shelter beneath the overhang of an empty shed and opened the ledger again, shielding it from the rain with my body. Marwood's handwriting was steady throughout, even where the entries grew darker. Names reduced to initials. Initials reduced to numbers. Numbers annotated, then crossed through.

Arthur Selwyn's line cut off.

Evelyn's did not.

She had come to Orford Ness not knowing the full shape of what Arthur had uncovered, only that he had stopped writing. Stopped sending money home. Stopped existing.

She had followed his work the way a careful woman follows a trail left by someone who assumed no one would ever look for it.

The camera plates had been the key.

Once she understood what Arthur had seen, she understood why he could not be allowed to speak.

And once she understood that, she understood her own danger.

Marwood had known this.

Hargreaves had known enough.

Pike had been instructed.

Containment, I saw now, was not a single act. It was a cascade—each decision justified by the one before it, each correction framed as necessity.

The storm intensified, thunder rolling across the Ness in sustained waves that made the ground itself seem to vibrate. The river surged against the wall, stones shifting under pressure not meant to be applied so soon.

The walls were closing in again.

Not just around me.

Around the truth.

Somewhere, Marwood was already beyond reach—moved inland, reassigned, folded into another facility where her calm would be useful and her conscience unnecessary. Somewhere else, Arthur Selwyn's images had been reduced to fragments, their existence denied, their implications buried under classification stamps and urgency.

And somewhere very close, men were deciding how much longer I could be permitted to remain a variable.

I did not wait for them to decide.

As the storm broke fully, I made my own preparations.

Truth cannot always be exposed by force. Sometimes it must be released—placed where containment no longer has jurisdiction, where systems cannot quietly correct it without drawing attention to themselves.

Arthur Selwyn had believed reporting was enough.

Evelyn had believed visibility was protection.

They had both been mistaken.

But they had not been foolish.

The Ness, dark and indifferent under the storm, did not care about aerial cameras or naval installations, or ledgers marked for erasure. It remembered only what had been done to it.

And now, so did I.

As I turned away from the airfield, the rain erased my footprints almost at once. The wall held—for now. The sheds loomed, empty of purpose. The camera that had seen too much was gone, but the image it had captured could not be unseen.

Arthur Selwyn had been right to be afraid.

And whoever thought the storm would finish this was about to learn the same lesson he had.

The higher you build your secrets, the farther they fall when the light finally reaches them.

22

The truth does not want to be told.

That was the lesson Arthur Selwyn learned too late, and Evelyn Selwyn learned in time to die for it. Truth resists exposure. It bends toward concealment, toward the nearest explanation that allows the world to keep its shape. If you let it, it will be smothered by language, classified into silence, or reduced to an error that can be corrected.

I stood at the edge of the Ness with the storm still pressing at my back and understood that the question was no longer *whether* the truth would survive.

It was the location where respiration would be permitted.

Whitehall was not an option.

That had been settled long before I arrived on Orford Ness, before Eleanor ever walked the marsh, before Arthur Selwyn traced forbidden lines on a wet photographic plate. Whitehall had already seen what the camera saw. It had simply chosen not to recognise it.

To send the truth upward through official channels would be to hand it back to the same system that had named murder *containment* and fear *procedure*.

The War Office would thank me for my diligence, mark my report *sensitive*, and bury it beneath a stamp heavy enough to crush memory itself.

No.

Evelyn had understood this.

That was why she never tried to report what she learned. She did not argue policy. She did not plead morality. She prepared an exit route for the evidence itself.

The Zeppelin.

I walked back toward the remains of the wreckage, now half-swallowed by water and shadow, and let the shape of it settle properly in my mind.

The crash had been an accident.

That much was now clear.

Weather, altitude, structural failure—any one of them could have brought the airship down. The Ness does not require malice to kill. It only requires opportunity.

But Evelyn's murder was not an accident.

She had been calm because she was ready. She had been walking because she had already chosen her deadline. The Zeppelin was not her escape; it was her courier.

She meant to send the truth *out* of Britain, not herself.

I understood now what she had tried to do.

The airship had been convenient not because it was German, but because it was *uncontrollable*. Enemy craft could not be officially inspected without awkward questions. What was hidden aboard it would be presumed hostile, not domestic. If the evidence reached the continent, it could not be quietly reclassified. It would have to be denied publicly—or explained.

And explanation was the one thing the system could not afford.

That was why she was killed.

Not in panic.

Not in rage.

But carefully.

Placed where fire and wreckage would do the rest.

I thought of Keller then—watching from above, seeing a woman argue with a man who believed he had authority over consequence. Seeing her stop, not because she agreed, but because she understood.

She knew Marwood had decided.

Dr Elspeth Marwood had not merely complied.

She had ordered.

Containment was not a suggestion scribbled in a ledger. It was an instruction carried out by men like Pike, justified by officers like Hargreaves, and sanctified by silence further up the chain.

Marwood had ordered Arthur Selwyn's erasure the moment he became inconvenient.

She had ordered Evelyn's the moment Evelyn refused to be frightened.

And now, she had ordered mine.

Not with a weapon.

With a designation.

Unstable.

Disloyal.

Obstructive.

Words that travel faster than truth and kill just as cleanly.

I was already contained in all but name.

The ledger lay heavy under my coat. The list was folded inside it, creased now from handling, the names pressed into the paper as though trying to elude it.

Arthur Selwyn.

Evelyn.

Others.

Too many.

I could not take this to London.

I could not keep it on the Ness.

And I could not trust it to remain with me for long.

Containment would come again, quieter this time, better prepared. Another accident. Another misstep. Another assessment of fitness.

The system corrected until it no longer needed to.

So I did what Evelyn had done.

I looked for a way out that did not ask permission.

The storm gave me cover. It flattened the world, blurred edges, made movement ordinary again. Men were too busy protecting equipment, files, reputations. No one was watching the marsh.

I made my way inland, keeping to the lowest ground, where the Ness had already begun to erase footprints. The river wall groaned behind me, stones shifting, the argument it represented finally collapsing into concession.

At the edge of the old supply track, I stopped and looked back once—not at the camp, but at the land itself.

The Ness did not care where the truth went.

It had already kept it long enough.

I knew where mine had to go.

Not to a desk.

Not to a committee.

But to a place where denial would be loud, public, and irreversible.

The press.

Neutral intermediaries.

Foreign eyes.

Places where questions could not be smothered without consequence.

Arthur had believed reporting was enough.

Evelyn had believed movement was protection.

I would do neither.

I would scatter the truth so widely that containment could no longer gather it again.

The ledger would be copied, then broken apart. The list would not travel whole. Names would surface in places that could not coordinate their disappearance.

If I were corrected, it would be too late.

I felt a sense of grief—not just for Evelyn, Arthur, or Keller, but also for the part of me that once thought exposure was an event, not an ongoing process.

Marwood had been right about one thing.

Truth is not innocent.

But she was mistaken about who decides its harm.

I turned away from Orford Ness and walked, keeping my pace unremarkable, my posture tired rather than urgent.

Because of that, too, Evelyn had understood.

The truth does not survive by being dramatic.

It survives by getting away.

And this time it would.

23

The plate was not meant to survive.

That much was obvious the moment I took it out of my pocket and laid it on the table. Even broken, even dulled by mishandling and time, it carried the stubbornness of something that had already decided not to disappear. The crack that ran through its centre had not erased the image beneath. It had merely interrupted it.

That was the danger of photographs.

They did not argue. They did not persuade. They simply insisted.

I was alone when I developed it. That mattered. There are moments when witnesses contaminate what they observe simply by wanting it to mean something. I did not want this to mean anything more than it already did.

The room I used was not a darkroom in the proper sense—no tiled walls, no purpose-built drains, no sign warning the careless away. It was a borrowed space behind a shuttered shop, inland, where damp was already a given and questions were not asked so long as the rent was paid on time. The window had been blacked out with heavy cloth. The door locked. The world reduced to chemical smell and waiting.

I laid out the tools carefully.

A shallow tray.

Fresh solution.

The plate, wrapped until now in oilcloth and caution.

My hands were steady.

That surprised me.

I had expected anger, or fear, or at least the tremor of anticipation. Instead, there was only focus—the kind that comes when the mind has already accepted what the eyes are about to confirm.

I slid the plate into the tray.

At first, there was nothing.

That is always how it begins. A blankness that invites doubt. You think the damage has been too severe, the emulsion too compromised, the truth too neatly erased.

Then the image emerged.

Slowly. Reluctantly. As though it had been waiting for the correct conditions rather than rescue.

The land came first.

The curve of the river.

The marsh edge.

The low ridge where the ground lifts just enough to give the illusion of safety.

The Ness.

Unmistakable, even flattened by height and distance. Even reduced to lines and shadows. The place has a grammar all its own.

I leaned closer.

The geometry resolved next—shapes that did not belong to water or erosion. Straight edges. Right angles. Human insistence interrupting the land's refusal. I recognised them at once, though I had never been meant to.

The installation.

Partially masked. Carefully aligned to deceive anything looking from the wrong height, at the wrong time, with the wrong instrument.

Arthur Selwyn had been the first to understand that mistake.

The plate darkened further.

Figures emerged.

Three of them.

One stood slightly apart, nearer the river, coat drawn close against the wind. Even blurred by scale, even distorted by the fracture running through the image, I knew her.

Evelyn.

Eleanor Selwyn.

She was not running. She was not crouched or concealed. She stood as someone stands when they expect to be heard. Her posture was upright her head turned toward the two figures facing her.

Two men.

One taller, shoulders rounded slightly forward, as though trying to occupy less space than his authority permitted. The other shorter, stance rigid, weight balanced too carefully to be casual.

Pike.

And another.

The crack in the plate cut across the second man's face, rendering his features unreadable. But posture is harder to disguise than expression. I recognised the angle of his shoulders, the way he stood angled away from the woman even as she faced him directly.

Authority, already withdrawing.

The image sharpened.

Evelyn's arm was raised.

Not in appeal.

In accusation.

Her hand struck Pike's chest.

Not violently.

Deliberately.

I held my breath without realising it.

The plate did not show what was said. It did not show the sound of wind across the marsh, or the distant thrum of machinery, or the knowledge passing between them that there would be no acceptable outcome.

But it showed sequence.

Evelyn confronting.

Pike listening.

The other man already disengaging.

The next frame—captured seconds later, perhaps minutes—told the rest.

Evelyn was no longer standing.

Her body lay at the edge of the reeds, one arm outstretched, her coat twisted at an angle that spoke of force rather than collapse. Pike stood over her, his posture altered now—not frantic, not panicked, but intent.

The other man was gone.

Already absent.

Already erased.

I let the plate rest in the solution until the image was fully developed, until there could be no argument about what it showed. Then I lifted it carefully, holding it up to the dim light.

Arthur Selwyn's murder had not been caught by the camera.

This was worse.

This was premeditation.

Evelyn had been killed not because she happened to be there, but because she refused to leave.

Because she had discovered what Arthur had seen and understood what it meant.

The Zeppelin had been her deadline.

Not her escape.

I thought of the wreckage then—the careful placement of her body, the absence of burn marks, the deliberate alignment that suggested respect rather than haste. Someone had wanted her hidden, not destroyed. Someone had believed the Ness would do the rest.

They had underestimated two things.

The land.

And the camera.

Arthur Selwyn had believed reporting was enough.

He had taken the plate to his superior, expecting escalation to mean correction. He had believed the system would repair itself if shown the flaw.

Instead, it repaired the witness.

Arthur's death was not an accident. It was not even a punishment. It was a resolution.

The experiment failed.

Arthur knew why.

And so he had to be contained.

I understood now why his body had been left where it fell, deep beneath the airfield. It was not laziness. It was certainty. Certainty that no one would ever look there again. Certainty that the chamber itself would become part of the denial.

And Evelyn?

Evelyn had learned from Arthur's mistake.

She made no effort to file a report.

She tried to move the evidence.

The Zeppelin was perfect.

Enemy craft. Uninspectable. Already guilty in the eyes of anyone who recovered it. If the plates reached the continent, the truth would no longer belong to Whitehall. It would have to be denied publicly.

Or explained.

The crash ruined that plan.

The Ness is unsympathetic to intention.

But her murder was not part of the crash.

It was part of the correction.

Dr Marwood had ordered it.

I saw that clearly now—not because her name appeared on a list, but because the logic was unmistakable. Pike had been the instrument. The other man, the witness. The decision had been made long before Evelyn walked onto the marsh.

Containment was not reactive.

It was anticipatory.

I removed the plate from the solution and set it aside to dry, propped at an angle that would allow no pooling, no distortion. I did not rush. Rushing was how mistakes were made.

I washed my hands slowly, letting the chemicals rinse away.

Then I sat.

And I thought.

The system had already decided what to do with me.

That much was clear.

I had been designated obstructive. Disloyal. Unstable. The paperwork would already be circulating, attaching itself to my name like a second skin. If I went back to London now, I would not be heard.

I would be assessed.

If I stayed where I was, I would be corrected.

Another fall.

Another accident.

Another muted explanation.

The plate changed that calculus.

This was not testimony.

This was not an interpretation.

This was an image of a British officer killing a British civilian on British soil to protect a secret installation that officially did not exist.

The truth did not need framing.

It needed distribution.

I returned to the plate once it had dried and wrapped it carefully. Then I took out the ledger and placed it beside it on the table.

Two kinds of proof.

One bureaucratic.

One incontrovertible.

Marwood had believed the list was sufficient.

She had been wrong.

Lists can be rewritten.

Images cannot.

I thought of Keller then—watching from above, already condemned by nationality and survival. He had seen the argument. He had spoken. And for that, he would be blamed.

Unless the truth reached somewhere his voice could not be dismissed as enemy invention.

The press.

Foreign attachés.

Neutral investigators.

Places where denial would have to be performed in daylight.

I did not need to send everything to one place.

That was another of Arthur's mistakes.

Truth survives best when it is broken into pieces small enough to be carried, large enough to be recognised.

The plate would go one way.

The ledger another.

The names would surface separately, each context forcing its own questions.

Containment depends on coordination.

I would deny them that.

I packed the materials carefully, separating them, wrapping each as though it were fragile—which, in a sense, it was. Paper burns. Glass shatters. Men fall.

But memory, once externalised, becomes harder to kill.

As I prepared to leave, I caught my reflection in the darkened window.

I looked tired.

Not unstable.

Not obsessed.

Just tired in the way men do when they have reached the end of observation and crossed into obligation.

I thought of Evelyn again—standing on the marsh, coat drawn tight, silk hidden beneath wool. Calm because she had already decided what mattered more than survival.

Arthur Selwyn had died because he believed in process.

Evelyn had died because she believed in exposure.

I would survive because I believed in escape.

Not of myself.

Of the truth.

I extinguished the light, locked the door, and stepped out into the night.

The Ness lay behind me, dark and patient.

It would remember.

But it no longer needed to keep the secret alone.

This time, the image would travel.

24

I saw her run.

That was the moment everything narrowed.

The storm had thickened into something purposeful by then, rain driven low across the Ness, flattening grass and scrub until the land seemed pressed into obedience. The sheds stood half-submerged in shadow, their outlines broken by rain and darkness, their doors banging softly as the wind worried at them like a persistent thought.

Marwood emerged from the hangar without hesitation.

No coat pulled tight. No glance over her shoulder. She moved with the certainty of someone who had already decided the shape of her escape. Her boots struck the concrete apron once, twice, then she was on the shingle, angling away from the airfield toward the dark sweep of the Ness.

Toward the water.

I followed.

I did not shout her name. I did not call for help. Sound travels too far on open ground, and there were ears here that did not belong to the storm.

She cut between the outer sheds, moving fast now, her silhouette briefly swallowed, then released again by the darkness. The rain blurred distance and distorted depth. The Ness has always been like that—making certainty provisional.

"Marwood," I called at last.

She did not slow.

Instead, she changed direction.

She slipped through the open doors of Shed Seven, one of the old testing buildings, long since stripped of its original purpose. I followed her inside and felt the world contract at once.

The air changed.

Oil and damp metal. Rust and old insulation. The smell of things that had been run too hard and then abandoned without ceremony. The rain drummed on the roof above us, amplified until it sounded like movement—like feet pacing in the dark.

My torch beam cut through the interior.

Racks stood empty where instruments had once been mounted. Cables trailed from the walls like veins severed mid-flow. A test rig loomed at the far end, its metal frame shifting slightly as the wind found gaps in the structure.

The shed groaned.

Not metaphorically.

Physically.

Steel expanding and contracting under temperature and strain, joints complaining, bolts clicking as though counting something out.

Marwood moved ahead of me, her footsteps precise even on the uneven floor.

"You should stop," she said without turning. Her voice carried easily, controlled, as though we were walking down a corridor rather than running through a collapsing building in a storm.

"I don't think so," I replied.

She laughed once, short and incredulous. "You're not equipped for this."

"For running?" I asked. "Or for listening?"

She reached the far door and shoved it open. Wind and rain burst in, flattening my torch beam into a smear of light.

"For understanding," she said.

We emerged into another stretch of open ground, this one narrower, hemmed in by sheds on either side. The testing area. Old scaffolds and frames stood like ribs against the dark, their shapes thrown grotesque by lightning.

She slowed here—not from fatigue, but calculation.

"You don't know how far up this goes," she said, raising her voice to carry over the storm.

"I know where it ends," I said. "With bodies."

She turned then, finally facing me.

The rain streaked her face, but her expression was unchanged. Calm. Focused. The composure of a woman who had survived by believing she was right.

"You think this is about murder," she said. "It isn't."

"You ordered it," I said. "Arthur. Evelyn. And now me."

Her eyes flicked, just once.

"I acted under orders," she said. "From above. From people you will never meet and could not recognise if you did."

"That doesn't absolve you."

"It explains it," she replied. "In war, explanation is the only currency."

Thunder rolled overhead, close enough to feel through the ground. One of the old rigs shifted, metal shrieking briefly before settling again.

"Arthur Selwyn discovered a catastrophic breach," she went on. "Aerial reconnaissance designed to out-see the enemy revealed our own vulnerability instead. A restricted naval installation. Exposed. Documented. Uncontainable."

"And he threatened to report it."

"He threatened to *force* it," she said. "To take it to Whitehall. To put it into circulation."

"Because that's what honest men do."

"Because that's what naïve men do," she snapped. The first crack in her calm. "Do you know what admitting that mistake would have done? Not to me. To the war?"

I said nothing.

She stepped back, rain hammering into her shoulders, and I saw then that she was edging sideways—toward the open shingle beyond the sheds.

"The War Office would rather bury a scandal," she said, "than explain how we photographed our own secrets from the sky."

"And Evelyn?" I asked.

Her mouth tightened.

"Evelyn's death was regrettable," she said. "But necessary."

Lightning split the sky, briefly freezing the world in hard white detail—the scaffolds, the cables, the water running in channels where no channels had been designed.

"She tried to smuggle the evidence out," Marwood continued. "Via the Zeppelin. Clever, really. Enemy craft.

Uninspectable. If the plates reached the continent, the truth would no longer belong to us."

"And when the Zeppelin crashed?"

"That was a coincidence," she said immediately. "Weather. Altitude. Structural failure. The Ness does not need help to kill machines."

"But her murder wasn't."

"No," Marwood said. "It was not."

The admission sat between us, clean and undeniable.

"You killed her," I said.

"I corrected a problem," she replied. "The same way engineers always do."

She turned and ran again.

This time she did not head back toward the airfield.

She went out onto the shingle.

The worst possible ground.

Loose stones shifted underfoot, each step an argument with gravity. The wind was stronger here, unimpeded by structures, driving rain sideways until it stung like grit.

I followed, boots slipping, lungs burning as the cold air cut deep.

Ahead, the darkness opened into a wider stretch of shore. I could hear the sea now—not the gentle breathing it had offered earlier, but a deeper, angrier sound. Waves striking shingle hard enough to be felt through the soles of my feet.

There was a boat.

Not visible yet, but I knew it was there. The way she angled her run gave it away. Purpose returns to the body when it sees an end.

"Stop," I called.

She did not.

We passed the last of the sheds, their hulks receding behind us, and the Ness opened wide—raw, exposed, indifferent. Lightning flickered again, and in that brief illumination I saw it: a small launch pulled up beyond the tideline, its silhouette dark against darker water.

A figure moved near it.

Waiting.

Marwood stumbled then.

Just for a moment.

The shingle shifted under her, treacherous as ever, and she went down hard, hands catching herself on stone. I closed the distance before she could rise.

She looked up at me, rain streaming down her face, eyes bright with something close to fury.

"You don't understand what you're doing," she said.

"I understand exactly," I replied. "You built a system that eats its own witnesses."

"And you think dragging this into the light will save anyone?" she demanded. "You think the War Office will thank you for exposing their mistakes in the middle of a war?"

"No," I said. "I think they'll hate me."

She laughed then, breathless and sharp. "Good. Because hatred is survivable. Irrelevance is not."

She twisted, trying to break free, but I had her wrist now, my grip firm despite the cold.

"The truth is already moving," I said. "You can't stop it."

Marwood looked past me, toward the waiting boat, toward whatever calculation had been waiting there.

"You're mistaken," she whispered. "It always stops. Eventually."

The figure by the boat raised an arm, signalling.

Marwood made one last effort to pull free.

I tightened my grip.

"No," I said. "This time it doesn't."

For a moment we stood there, rain hammering down, the sea roaring its disapproval, the Ness watching as it always had.

Then voices rose behind us—shouts, indistinct, carried by the wind. Lights flickered at the edge of the airfield, torches cutting erratic paths through the dark.

The walls were closing in.

On both of us.

Marwood looked at me, really looked, and something shifted in her expression—not fear, but recognition.

"You're going to make this impossible," she said.

"I know," I replied.

She went still, then the fight leaving her, shoulders sagging as though she had finally reached the limit of what certainty could carry.

Behind us, the storm continued its work, erasing footprints, flattening evidence, refusing to care who was right.

But the truth no longer needed the Ness to keep it.

25

The wall did not fail all at once.

It never does.

It argued first.

I heard it before I saw it—stone shifting against stone, a low, grinding sound beneath the wind, like teeth worrying a bone. The river pressed harder than it had the night before, swollen with rain, its surface no longer sliding but surging, testing each course of rock as if reading the workmanship aloud.

The storm had not lessened. It had simply settled into itself.

I reached the bend just as the labourers were being herded back into place, their coats already dark with water, their boots slick with mud and shingle. The wall ran along the river's uncertain edge like a stitched wound—never meant to heal, only to be held together long enough to look convincing.

Liang Wei was there.

I recognised him by the way he stood, not braced, not panicked, but attentive, his weight balanced as though he were listening through his feet. Our eyes met for a moment, and in that fleeting exchange, I realised that everything occurring now had been foreseen.

"The water has memory," he said, raising his voice over the wind. "It knows where it has been."

The men were passing stones hand to hand, forming a line that bent and reshaped itself as the river pressed in. Their movements were efficient, practiced. No wasted motion. No talk.

They did not look like soldiers.

They looked like men accustomed to being unseen.

The foreman shouted instructions, his voice sharp with effort, but it carried no authority the water recognised. A stone slipped. Another set to replace it. Mortar bled out, pale against the dark.

The wall sagged.

Not dramatically.

Just enough.

The river surged, slipped through a seam, then pulled back, as if tasting.

I stepped closer, boots sinking into the saturated ground, and felt the vibration through the soles—pressure translating itself into movement.

This was not engineering.

It was a negotiation.

"You should not be here," the foreman shouted at me.

I did not answer.

I was watching the water.

Watching the point where the river leaned hardest, where the stones had been scavenged from older foundations, where the Ness was reclaiming its own materials with methodical patience.

Liang moved beside me.

"They were told to finish this quickly," he said. "Too quickly."

"By whom?" I asked.

He did not answer.

He did not need to.

A shout went up further down the wall. One of the men stumbled as a stone shifted under his foot. Two others grabbed him before he went into the water. The river surged again, higher this time, breaking white against the base of the wall.

The argument was ending.

I felt it then—not fear, but certainty.

Marwood would not wait for the outcome.

She would already be moving.

I turned away from the wall and scanned the airfield beyond it the storm flattening distance, turning sheds and hangars into dark suggestions rather than structures. Lights flickered, some extinguished entirely. Men ran between buildings, their outlines bent by rain and urgency.

The camp was responding.

But not uniformly.

Some movement was defensive. Some was evasive.

And some—one line of motion in particular—was deliberate.

I saw it then.

A figure moving along the outer track, keeping to the lee of the sheds, angling away from the main cluster of buildings and toward the open shingle beyond.

Purpose has a rhythm.

Once you know it, you can hear it even in a storm.

Marwood.

The wall gave another shudder behind me, a longer one this time, stones shifting as a section bowed inward. The labourers shouted now, not in panic but in coordination, their voices overlapping as they tried to reinforce the failing seam.

Liang caught my sleeve.

"She will not wait for this," he said.

"I know," I replied.

I started toward the sheds.

Behind me, the wall groaned, and the river surged through the gap with sudden force, water spilling across the worksite, washing tools and loose stones downstream. The men scrambled back, boots slipping, coats dragging them down.

The foreman shouted again, but the sound was lost to the water.

The wall had lost the argument.

I ran.

Not blindly.

Not quickly enough to draw attention.

The sheds loomed ahead, dark hulks against the storm, their doors banging and rattling as the wind found purchase. These were the testing sheds—the ones that had once housed instruments, rigs, machines meant to see farther than men were comfortable with.

Now they housed only echoes.

I cut between two of them and felt the world narrow again, the open chaos of the river replaced by something tighter, more intimate. The storm sounded different here, broken by walls and metal, rain hammering into roofs and running down gutters that no longer bothered to direct it anywhere useful.

I saw her slip into Shed Four.

I followed.

Inside, the darkness was complete for a moment, the torch beam swallowed by dust and rain and hanging shadows. Then the light found shape.

Racks.

Frames.

Cables swaying like vines.

The machinery groaned as the wind pushed against the structure, metal complaining as though remembering what it had once been asked to do. A rig shifted, chains clinking softly, the sound too close to breathing to be comfortable.

"Dr Marwood," I called.

No answer.

I moved deeper, boots splashing through pooled water on the floor. Something crunched underfoot—glass, perhaps, or old ceramic insulation. The beam caught fragments of chalk markings on the walls, half-erased numbers, and symbols that meant nothing now, or meant too much.

She emerged at the far end of the shed, already at the door.

"You're persistent," she said, her voice calm despite the storm.

"You're running," I replied.

She paused, one hand on the doorframe, rain streaking her coat, her hair finally loosened by the wind.

"I'm leaving," she corrected. "There's a difference."

"For you," I said.

"For everyone," she replied.

She stepped out into the storm again, and I followed, the door slamming behind me with a sound like punctuation.

The shingle stretched ahead, pale and shifting, the river now roaring somewhere to my left as it reclaimed the worksite. The wall was no longer holding; water was spilling freely now, cutting channels where none had been planned.

Marwood moved with care across the loose stone, adjusting her pace, choosing her footing. She knew this ground well enough to respect it.

I matched her distance, close enough not to lose her, far enough not to force her into panic.

Ahead, the darkness opened.

The sound of the sea rose—deeper than the river, angrier, waves striking shingle with enough force to be felt through the ground.

There was a boat.

I did not need to see it to know.

The angle of her path told me everything.

"You won't make it," I called.

She did not turn.

"I don't need to," she replied. "I just need to be gone."

Lightning split the sky, illuminating the shore in hard white detail. For an instant I saw it clearly: a small launch pulled up beyond the tideline, its outline low and purposeful, a figure waiting beside it, shoulders hunched against the weather.

An arrangement.

Not an improvisation.

"This ends now," I said.

She stopped then.

Turned.

The rain ran down her face, her eyes bright, not with fear but with resolve sharpened into something harder.

"No," she said. "This ends when it's contained."

"You ordered my containment," I said.

"Yes," she replied, without hesitation. "Because you would not stop."

"And Arthur?" I asked.

She did not look away.

"Arthur Selwyn threatened to force disclosure," she said. "That could not be permitted."

"And Evelyn?"

A flicker, then gone.

"Evelyn Selwyn refused to be frightened," she said. "That made her dangerous."

"You murdered her," I said.

"I corrected a breach," she replied. "The same way I was trained to."

The wind surged again, nearly knocking us both off balance. Behind us, a section of the river wall collapsed completely, the sound carrying even over the storm—a deep, grinding roar as stone and water surrendered to gravity.

The Ness reclaiming.

"She tried to send the evidence out," I said. "On the Zeppelin."

Marwood nodded. "Yes."

"And the crash?"

"A coincidence," she said. "Structural failure. Weather. Probability."

"But her death wasn't."

"No," she agreed. "It was necessary."

The simplicity of it was almost worse than denial.

"You think the War Office will protect you," I said.

"I know they will," she replied. "They will protect the war. I am incidental."

She took a step backward toward the waiting boat.

"They will bury this," she went on. "They will say the camera malfunctioned. That Selwyn was unstable. That you interfered. That a storm destroyed the rest."

"They'll be incorrect," I said.

"They'll be believed," she replied.

Another wave struck the shore, closer now, spraying us both with cold water. The figure by the boat raised an arm, signalling again, more urgently this time.

Marwood turned.

I moved.

I caught her arm as she stepped, my grip sliding on wet fabric before finding purchase. She staggered, nearly falling, then twisted, trying to wrench free.

"You don't understand," she said, breath sharp now. "This isn't about truth. It's about survival."

"Not yours," I said.

"Not yours either," she shot back.

We stood there, locked together, the storm howling, the river roaring behind us, the wall's failure echoing through the ground like an aftershock.

For a moment, I thought she might strike me.

Instead, she went still.

"You can't stop what's coming," she whispered. "You can only decide how many people it takes with it."

"I've already decided," I replied.

Behind us, voices rose—shouts, torches cutting through the rain as men moved toward the shore. The camp was responding now, late but inevitably.

Marwood looked past me, toward the lights, toward the collapsing wall, toward the labourers scrambling to higher ground.

Then she laughed.

Not loudly.

Almost fondly.

"You think the wall failed by accident," she said.

"What do you mean?" I asked.

She met my gaze.

"Containment always leaks," she said. "Water just makes it obvious."

The figure by the boat lowered his arm.

The launch remained where it was.

The storm pressed in, erasing footprints, flattening paths, refusing to care who had been right or wrong.

The Ness did not choose sides.

It remembered.

And as the river poured through the broken wall and the sheds groaned behind us, I understood something I had not fully grasped until now.

Marwood was not escaping the storm.

She was being overtaken by it.

And so was everything else that had been hidden here.

26

The wall had become a corridor.

Not by design—by failure.

It ran along the river's edge in a low, broken line, stones set too quickly and mortar already bleeding out, and now the storm used it as a funnel. Water pressed against it from one side, wind from the other, and men moved along it as though it were still a structure rather than an argument in the process of losing.

I followed Marwood onto it because there was nowhere else to go.

The shore to our right had become treacherous shingle, shifting and sliding underfoot. The river to our left was a dark, muscular thing, swollen with rain, shouldering stones aside as if offended by the attempt to tell it where to run. Behind us, the camp lights bucked and blurred through sheets of water, torches cutting frantic arcs that meant nothing at this distance.

Ahead, the darkness opened toward the mouth of the river and the sea beyond it—toward the waiting boat I had glimpsed in lightning, a small launch pulled beyond the tideline like a thought held back only by timing.

The wall did not fail with a single dramatic gesture.

It failed in increments, like a story being rewritten sentence by sentence.

A stone shifted under my boot and rolled into the water with a dull, last sound. Another loosened near my ankle, tilting the line by a fraction. The river surged in, tasting the gap, then pulled back as if deciding whether to swallow the rest at once or take it piece by piece.

Marwood moved ahead of me, her silhouette narrowing in the rain, a woman reduced to motion.

She did not look back.

She did not need to.

Everything behind her was already closing.

Her boots found purchase with careful efficiency. She knew how to move across unstable ground. Engineers understand load and failure and the ways structures announce themselves before collapse. She ran along the wall as if she had built it, as if she owned it, as if the river was merely another variable to be managed.

I kept my distance at first. Close enough not to lose her, far enough not to force her into panic.

Panic makes noise.

Noise invites attention.

The storm was already loud enough.

Lightning split the sky, hard and white, and for an instant the world froze into exactness: the wall's uneven spine; the river's churning black; the reeds flattened like hair combed by a brutal hand. And ahead—there it was again—the boat, low and purposeful, a figure waiting near it, shoulders hunched against weather that could not be negotiated with.

Then the darkness closed again, and the storm resumed its work.

Marwood's path angled not toward the boat directly, but toward the point where the wall dipped closest to the river mouth, where the bank narrowed and the water ran faster, where stepping off the stones would be a single decision between salvage and submersion.

She was not fleeing blindly.

She was moving toward an exit she had measured.

I tightened my grip on the ledger under my coat and felt the folded list press against my ribs like a reminder that paper can cut.

"Marwood!" I called.

The wind stole half the name, flung it back into my mouth.

She slowed, only slightly. Enough to prove she had heard.

"Lieutenant," she said without turning, as though addressing an inconvenience that refused to remain filed. "This is absurd."

"Stop," I said.

"Stop where?" she asked, still facing forward. "On a wall that's collapsing? In a storm? On a coast that eats anything it's given?"

Her voice remained calm, and that calm was the most frightening thing of all. Panic would have been human. Anger would have been recognisable. But Marwood spoke as if we were discussing tolerances in a lab, not the moral weight of dead bodies.

"You're heading for a boat," I said.

She laughed once—short, almost pitying. "You're very observant."

"I'm out of time for your lessons," I said.

"You were out of time the moment you decided to be righteous," she replied.

A section of the wall groaned beneath us—a low grinding shift as stones settled into a new, worse arrangement. The river surged against the base, white breaking through a seam that had not been there a moment before.

The wall was not merely failing.

It was being dismantled with patience.

The Ness does not hurry. It does not need to.

"Arthur Selwyn is in the ground beneath your airfield," I said. "Or what's left of it."

Marwood did not turn, but I saw her shoulders tighten under the rain.

"Arthur Selwyn is in the past," she said. "Where he belongs."

"Evelyn isn't," I said. "Neither is Eleanor. Neither is Keller. Neither am I."

At that, she stopped.

Not abruptly. Not fearfully. Like a woman deciding the discussion had reached a point where it required eye contact.

She turned on the wall, careful with her footing, the storm pulling at her coat as if trying to strip away her composure. Rain ran down her face. Lightning lit her eyes for a fraction of a second, making them look pale and empty, like glass held to light.

"Do you know what you're doing?" she asked.

"Yes," I said. "I'm preventing you from leaving."

Her mouth tightened. "You can't prevent anything," she said. "You can only alter how much collateral it creates."

The river struck the base of the wall again, harder. The stones shuddered underfoot. Somewhere behind us, a shout rose—thin and distant, swallowed by wind.

The camp was responding late, and late responses are always messy.

Marwood looked past me toward the distant lights, the men moving like insects around a thing they no longer controlled.

"They'll blame you," she said. "Or they'll call you ill. Or they'll call you disloyal. It's all the same end with different paperwork."

"And you?" I asked. "What will they call you?"

"Irrelevant," she said. "And that is survivable."

"You killed her," I said. "Don't hide behind language."

She didn't flinch.

"I corrected a breach," she said, as if the words were interchangeable with morality. "She made herself unsustainable."

"She was your casualty," I said.

"She was your problem," Marwood replied. "And your solution. You just don't like how it looks."

The wall shifted again. A stone near Marwood's heel rolled outward and dropped into the river. She adjusted automatically, balance perfect, weight redistributed with engineering efficiency.

I envied it bleakly.

Men like Pike shook because they understood they were disposable.

Marwood did not shake because she believed she wasn't.

"Why run?" I asked. "If you believe you're right, why run at all?"

"Because being right doesn't protect you from idiots," she said. "And tonight the camp is full of them."

A gust struck, stronger than the rest, and for a moment the world leaned sideways. The river's roar rose, the wall's line blurred, and I had the sensation that the Ness itself was shifting its attention from people to physics.

Marwood lifted her chin slightly, tasting the air like an animal.

"The wall is going," she said, almost conversationally.

"Yes," I said. "It is."

"And so are you," she replied. "Unless you choose otherwise."

I stepped forward, careful, boots testing each stone. "You're not leaving," I said.

Marwood's eyes held mine, calm sharpening into something colder.

"Do you want the truth?" she asked.

"I already have it," I said.

"No," she replied softly. "You have a story. And stories can be contained. Truth survives when no one can agree how to describe it."

Lightning cracked again, and in the white flash her face looked carved rather than human.

"The War Office ordered it," she said.

The words landed with the weight of inevitability, not surprise.

I did not let myself react. Reaction is what men like her look for. It tells them where to press next.

"Ordered what?" I asked.

"The cover," she said. "The removal. The correction." She glanced toward the river as if it were a clock. "Arthur. Evelyn. The plates. The ledger. All of it."

"And you obeyed," I said.

"I implemented," she corrected, as though the distinction mattered. "Orders arrive. Work happens. That is how nations survive wars."

"And murder?" I said.

She looked at me as if I had asked whether rain was wet.

"Murder is a civilian word," she said. "This is national security."

I felt the ledger under my coat, the list inside it, the names written in ink that had survived water and darkness and a collapsing world.

"You're telling me this now to buy time," I said.

Marwood's mouth twitched. "You're learning," she said. "That's a pity."

A stone beneath my left foot shifted, and the wall sagged. I moved my weight quickly, but the motion loosened another seam. Water surged through, foaming briefly as it found purchase.

Marwood stepped back a pace, not away from me, but toward the point where the wall narrowed—toward her exit.

I matched her.

The wall between us and the sea was now a thin, unreliable line. On one side, the river. On the other, shingle sliding into black water. Behind, the camp lights blurred, distant, irrelevant.

The world reduced to two people and a failing structure.

"What did Eleanor know?" I asked.

"She knew enough," Marwood said. "Too much. She had Arthur's curiosity and none of his caution."

"She was his sister," I said.

"She was his consequence," Marwood replied.

"You marked her for containment," I said.

"I marked a variable," she said, voice still level. "She gave herself a name that mattered. Evelyn. Eleanor. It makes no difference. Names are for sentiment. We work with outcomes."

"And Pike?" I asked.

Marwood's gaze flicked, almost imperceptibly, toward the river bend—toward the stain Liang had shown me, toward the place the watch had been found.

"Pike was a tool," she said. "Tools shake when they realise they can be discarded."

"And Hollis?" I asked.

"Hollis watches," she said. "That's why he's useful. Witnesses are always useful until they aren't."

I moved another step forward. The stones under my boot were slick now, water running over them, turning the wall into a narrow bridge.

"You ordered my containment," I said.

Marwood's eyes met mine. "Yes," she said. "Because you are persistent. And persistence is contagious."

She spoke the next words with a calm that made my stomach turn.

"The War Office would rather sacrifice one lieutenant than risk a scandal that compromises the war effort."

"Compromises," I said.

"Exposes," she corrected. "Exposure is the enemy of survival."

The river surged again, harder. The wall shuddered beneath us.

A crack sounded—a sharp, sudden fracture-like bone.

Stones shifted in a chain, settling into a new configuration that was less a wall than a series of stepping points held together by water pressure and habit.

Marwood glanced down.

For the first time, I saw something like uncertainty pass through her expression.

Not fear.

Calculation becoming incomplete.

"You won't make the boat," I said.

She looked up again, calm returning like a mask drawn tight.

"You still believe this ends with a confession," she said. "You still believe someone will listen if you carry the right evidence to the right desk."

"I believe the truth has weight," I said.

"And I believe weight can be thrown into water," she replied.

She stepped sideways then, not toward me but toward the last intact section of wall leading to the river mouth. She was trying to slip past, to use the collapsing stones as cover.

I lunged.

Not violently. Not dramatically. I simply reached out and caught her sleeve.

The fabric tore slightly under my fingers, wet cloth giving way.

Marwood stumbled.

For the first time, the calm broke—not into panic, but into something close to irritation.

"Let go," she said.

"No," I replied.

Her boot slid on the stone. She windmilled an arm to regain balance. The river struck the base of the wall at that exact moment, not as a wave but as a shove, a sudden surge that lifted the structure and shifted it an inch sideways.

An inch was enough.

The stone under Marwood's foot rolled.

Her heel slipped.

She went down hard, not onto the wall but off it—tilting sideways toward the river, arms flailing, the line of her body suddenly human in its helplessness.

I grabbed for her.

My hand caught her wrist, slick with rain, fingers closing around bone.

For a moment, we were connected by a single point of contact: me braced on the wall, her weight pulling downward, the river hungry beneath her.

Her eyes widened—not in fear of death, but in anger at physics.

"You can't—" she began.

"Be quiet," I said, and hauled.

The wall shifted under my feet. Another stone dropped away. The river surged higher, licking the edge where Marwood's shoulder struck water.

She was heavier than she looked. Or perhaps I was weaker than I wanted to admit. My shoulder screamed in protest—the same shoulder that had struck stone in the dark, the same shoulder the medic had prodded and pronounced serviceable.

Serviceable is not the same as strong.

"Give me your other hand," I said.

Marwood's free hand clawed at the wall, fingers scraping wet stone, finding nothing but slime and movement.

The river pulled at her coat, trying to take it as payment.

"I can't—" she said again, breath ragged now.

"Yes, you can," I said. "Unless you want to drown."

Her eyes met mine.

And in them, for the first time, I saw fear.

Not fear of death.

Fear of being seen dying.

Fear of becoming an uncontrolled outcome.

She reached.

Her fingers found my sleeve. Gripped. Slid. Found again.

I pulled with everything I had left.

The wall groaned.

A section behind me collapsed with a deep grinding roar, stones tumbling into the river, water rushing through the gap as if the wall had never existed at all.

The sound was immense.

It was the sound of an argument ending.

The shift disrupted my balance. My boot slipped. My knee slammed into stone. Pain flared white, then dulled.

I tightened my grip on Marwood's wrist, refusing to let go.

For a heartbeat, I thought I could haul her up.

At that point, the river determined its course of action.

A surge came—not a gentle rise, but a sudden, cold shove, as though the tide itself had taken offence at being resisted.

Water slammed against Marwood's torso, twisting her sideways. Her wrist jerked in my grasp, bone grinding under my fingers.

She gasped.

Not from cold.

From understanding.

"No," I said, though I do not know whether I meant her or the river.

Marwood's mouth opened as if to speak, but the wind stole the first sound.

I leaned further over the edge, extending myself dangerously, trying to use my own weight as leverage.

The ledger under my coat pressed painfully into my ribs.

A reminder of what I carried.

A reminder of what I might lose.

"Hold on!" I shouted.

Marwood's grip on my sleeve tightened, then loosened, then tightened again, fingers slipping on soaked cloth.

She looked up at me then.

Not pleading.

Not apologising.

She fulfilled her decision just before the water claimed her.

"You still don't know..." she said, voice thin against the storm.

Another surge hit her.

She swallowed water, coughed, fought for breath.

I pulled again, muscles burning.

She shook her head once—small, almost imperceptible.

"...who gave the order," she finished.

The words were not a confession.

They were a weapon.

A final correction.

Her fingers slipped from my sleeve.

For an instant I caught only cloth, then nothing at all.

Marwood fell backward into the tide, the river taking her with the blunt decisiveness of physics. She vanished beneath the surface, a dark shape swallowed by darker water.

I stared at the spot where she had been, as though staring could turn absence into return.

The river did not oblige.

It carried her away.

I fell back onto the wall, chest heaving, rain striking my face like blows. My hands shook now—not with fear of her, but with the delayed shock of what I had tried to do.

Save the woman who had ordered deaths.

Save the woman who had called murder procedure.

Save the woman who had tried to erase me.

And still, I had reached.

Because I had not become what they were.

Not yet.

The wall beneath me shifted again. More stones slid into the river with a sound like teeth loosening. The structure was going. The river was gradually absorbing the rest systematically, without intent or bias.

Behind me, shouts. Lights. Men approaching along the bank, too late to matter.

Ahead, the sea roared.

Somewhere near the tideline, the waiting boat's outline blurred in lightning and darkness. I could not tell if it had moved, if it had waited, if it had been there at all or had only been a promise.

The storm was unsympathetic.

It erased footprints. It drowned voices. It made every plan provisional.

Marwood was gone.

But her last sentence remained, lodged behind my ribs like the edge of a broken plate.

You still don't know who gave the order.

I looked down at my hands.

They were empty.

The river had taken her.

The Ness had taken the wall.

And somewhere beyond the storm—somewhere higher than Marwood, higher than Pike, higher than Hargreaves—someone still sat in a room and decided which truths were survivable.

The ground remembers.

But it does not name names.

That part was left to me.

I rose carefully, testing the stones with each step, and made my way back along what remained of the wall, the storm at my back and the weight of the unknown order pressing harder than the rain.

Because now the question was no longer whether I could prove what had happened.

I could.

The question was whether I could prove who had decided it should happen at all.

And how far they would go to ensure I never did.

27

The storm finished what men had begun.

It did not do so dramatically. There was no single moment that could be pointed to later and named as the end. It worked instead through accumulation—water where water should not have been, pressure applied long enough to become movement, weight transferred from one place to another until balance ceased to be a concept anyone could rely upon.

By dawn, the airfield was no longer pretending to be intact.

I saw it first from the rise above the Ness, where the land opens just enough to give the illusion of oversight. The runways lay scored and broken, long pale scars filled with standing water that reflected the low, exhausted sky. Canvas hangars slumped like men settling gently rather than collapsing. One of the smaller sheds had collapsed entirely, its roof folded in on itself, timbers snapped, iron ribs exposed to the rain.

The river had not returned to its old course.

It never does.

Where the wall had been, there was now a widening mouth, a place where the water had decided it preferred to go. Stones lay scattered downstream, some half-buried in mud, others carried farther than I would have believed possible. The labourers' tools were gone. Swept away. Claimed without comment.

The Ness had adjusted.

Men were already moving among the wreckage when I reached the perimeter. They did not run. Running would have suggested urgency. Instead, they walked with purpose, pointing, lifting, dragging. Damage was being translated into language that could be reported.

Structural compromise.

Storm damage.

Unavoidable loss.

I saw Pike near the ruined hangar, his coat collar turned up, his posture stiff. He spoke to an officer I did not recognise, gesturing once toward the river, then away again, as though the water were an embarrassment rather than a cause.

He did not look at me.

That told me enough.

The Zeppelin wreckage was being dealt with.

Not examined.

Not mourned.

Dealt with.

Teams of men worked around it with hooks and ropes, pulling loose fabric free, cutting away what remained of the envelope, separating the frame from the ground with an efficiency that spoke of rehearsal. The huge aluminium ribs were stacked like bones, their scale diminished by proximity. The scorched silk was folded, bundled, and carried off in sections, each one reduced to a manageable size.

Evidence shrinks when you break it apart.

The place where Evelyn's body had lain was already unrecognisable. Water had moved through it, smoothing the ground, erasing the slight depression where flesh had once displaced mud. Had I not been aware of the specific location to observe, I likely would have proceeded missing any irregularities.

The Ness remembers.

But it does not preserve.

Men remember differently.

They arrived just after noon.

Not in haste. Not with fanfare.

A pair of unmarked cars on the inland road, tyres crunching over shingle, stopped short of the major site as though unwilling to enter fully into what they saw. The men who stepped out wore civilian coats over uniforms that did not need to be visible to be recognised. Their manner was calm, their movements economical.

London made flesh.

The War Office did not announce itself. It did not need to. Authority announces itself by the way others step aside.

Hargreaves met them halfway, his expression arranged into something that suggested competence rather than relief. He spoke first, gesturing toward the damage, the river, the collapsed wall. He did not gesture toward the Zeppelin.

That omission was deliberate.

One of the men—a tall figure with a narrow face and eyes that seemed to take in everything without committing to reaction—listened without interrupting. When Hargreaves finished, he nodded once.

"Unfortunate," he said.

"Yes, sir," Hargreaves replied.

"And unavoidable?"

"Entirely."

The man looked toward the river then, watching the water move through its new channel with quiet interest.

"Nature has a way of complicating plans," he said.

"Indeed, sir."

The man turned his gaze at last toward the airfield proper. "And the investigation?"

Hargreaves hesitated only a fraction of a second. "Concluded," he said. "Pending formal review."

"Good," the man replied. "We want to make sure the conclusion is consistent."

I did not approach them.

Not yet.

There comes a time when influence emerges, and the best approach is to stand out without overwhelming others. To exist within the frame without demanding attention. I had learned that lesson early, and it had served me well enough to get this far.

They would come to me.

They always did.

The clearing continued around us. The Zeppelin's remains were loaded onto lorries, each piece recorded, each destination known only to those who would not be asked to remember it later. Men with clipboards moved among the work crews, their pens scratching steadily, transforming wreckage into inventory.

One of the War Office men—shorter, broader, his face already sliding toward anonymity—broke away from the group and approached me.

"Lieutenant Quirk," he said.

"Yes."

"You were on site during the incident?"

"I was."

"And during the storm."

"Yes."

He glanced at my boots, still stained with mud that had dried in irregular patterns. "You've been ... active."

"I've been present."

He smiled thinly. "Presence can be a liability."

"So I'm learning."

He gestured toward one of the remaining huts. "We'll need a statement."

"Of course."

Inside, the hut smelled of damp canvas and cold tea. A table had been cleared. Two chairs set opposite one another. The window had been wiped clean enough to allow light in, though not enough to offer any view worth having.

The tall man from before entered last and closed the door behind him.

"Lieutenant," he said, extending a hand I did not take. "I'm instructed to thank you for your service."

"Am I finished?" I asked.

He smiled again, that same expression of polite regret. "That depends on what you intend to say."

I sat.

They asked about the storm first. About the wall. About the labourers. I told them what could be seen. I described the water's pressure, the way the stones had shifted, the inevitability of collapse. I did not embellish. The truth did not require it.

They nodded, made notes.

Then they asked about the Zeppelin.

I described the crash. The fire. The wreckage. The recovery. I spoke carefully, choosing words that could not be rearranged later to mean something else. They listened without interruption.

Finally, they asked about Dr Marwood.

"When did you last see her?" the tall man asked.

"During the storm."

"Where?"

"On the Ness."

"In what capacity?"

"Running."

The shorter man looked up sharply. The tall one did not.

"And where is she now?" he asked.

"I don't know."

"That's unfortunate," the shorter man said.

"Is it?" I replied.

The tall man raised a hand, silencing him. "Lieutenant," he said, "Dr Marwood was reassigned prior to the storm. Her absence is already accounted for."

I met his gaze. "Then someone should tell the river."

Silence followed.

Not the Ness's silence. The human kind. Calculating.

"You're tired," the tall man said, eventually. "You've been through an ordeal."

"Yes."

"And in such circumstances," he continued, "memory can become ... unreliable."

I thought of Marwood's last words, carried away by water that was unsympathetic who had given the order.

"I remember clearly," I said.

"Memory," he replied, "is not the same as evidence."

I smiled then. I could not help it.

"No," I said. "But sometimes it outlives it."

The interview ended shortly after that. They did not press me. They did not need to. Pressure is most effective when applied elsewhere.

When I stepped outside, the clearing was nearly complete. Only a few pieces of the Zeppelin remained, too large to move quickly, their edges dulled by ash and rain. The place where it had fallen already looked emptier, as though it were being returned to its previous state by degrees.

A man approached me from the riverbank.

Liang Wei.

He looked exhausted his coat soaked through, his hands raw from cold and work. He did not speak at first. He simply stood beside me and watched the water move.

"They will say the wall was poorly built," he said at last.

"Yes."

"They will not say why it was rushed."

"No."

"They will not say why we were told to work through the night."

"No."

He nodded, accepting this without surprise. "The ground will remember," he said.

"Yes."

He glanced toward the place where the wall had been. "But it does not speak."

"No," I agreed. "That part is left to us."

The War Office cars departed shortly after. No sirens. No hurry. They had what they needed—or believed they did. The camp reformed around the new reality, lines redrawn, responsibilities reassigned.

By evening, the Ness looked almost peaceful again.

That, I knew, was the most dangerous moment of all.

Because calm invites forgetting.

I walked back toward the river as the light faded, stopping at the point where Marwood had fallen. There was nothing to mark it now. The water moved past without hesitation, carrying with it whatever it had been given.

"You still don't know who gave the order."

The words returned to me, insistent.

She had been right.

Names had not been spoken.

Only structures.

Only procedures.

Only necessity.

That was how systems survived: by ensuring that responsibility was always elsewhere.

I took the ledger from my coat and held it a moment, feeling its weight, the pressed paper, the names that had not yet found a place to rest.

The storm had destroyed part of the airfield.

The Zeppelin wreckage was gone.

The War Office had arrived.

And yet, nothing was finished.

Not really.

Because the truth was no longer here.

It was already moving.

And wherever it went, the water would follow, patient and unpersuaded, eroding certainty one stone at a time.

The Ness had done its part.

28

They brought the paper to me at dusk.

Not ceremonially. Not even with hostility. It arrived the way decisions of this sort always do—already settled, already formatted, accompanied by the mild expectation that I would complete the final, unnecessary gesture.

I was in the temporary office they had assigned me after the storm, a hut that smelled of damp wood and old ink, its windows wiped just clean enough to remind you there was a world outside you were no longer meant to influence. My coat hung over the back of the chair, still streaked with salt and mud. I had not bothered to clean it. There seemed little point in presenting myself as orderly when the situation itself had no interest in the truth.

The man who entered did not knock.

He wore a civilian coat over his uniform, the sort of compromise that suggests flexibility while concealing authority. He carried a folder under one arm, thin, efficient, its edges already softened by use.

"Lieutenant Quirk," he said, as though we were meeting for the first time.

"Yes."

He placed the folder on the desk between us and opened it without invitation. The paper inside was neatly typed, margins exact, language smoothed until no single sentence could be accused of urgency or care.

"Statement of Findings," it read.

I scanned the page once.

Then again.

I already knew what it would say. I had known since the moment the War Office cars arrived and the wreckage shrunk into manageable pieces.

Cause of death: injuries sustained during airship crash.

Contributory factors: fire, structural collapse, secondary impact.

No evidence of foul play.

Evelyn Selwyn's name appeared only once.

And not as a person.

As an inconvenience resolved by gravity and flame.

The man watched me read, his expression neutral in the way that passes for politeness among those who do not expect disagreement.

"This document summarises the agreed conclusion," he said. "It will be circulated to the relevant departments once signed."

I looked up.

"And if it isn't?"

He smiled, a small, patient thing. "Then it remains incomplete."

The implication hung between us, clean and unmistakable.

I turned another page.

My name appeared at the bottom.

Silas Quirk, Lieutenant.
Witness.

There was a space for my signature.

"You want me to say she died in the crash," I said.

"We want you to confirm the findings," he replied. "Language matters."

"She was murdered," I said.

The man's smile did not change, but something behind it cooled.

"You have been through a great deal," he said. "Fatigue can distort perception."

I laughed then.

Not loudly.

Just once.

"You cleared the wreckage," I said. "You washed the ground. You moved the body. And now you want my hand to tidy the rest."

He closed the folder gently, as though protecting it from insult.

"The war does not benefit from ambiguity," he said. "Nor from the reputational damage of speculation."

"This isn't speculation."

"No," he agreed. "It's interference."

I stood.

The chair scraped softly across the floor, an ordinary sound that felt indecently loud in the small room.

"She was alive before the Zeppelin fell," I said. "Seen by witnesses. She argued with a British officer. She was strangled and placed in the wreckage afterward."

His eyes flickered, just once.

"That is not the official account."

"It's the true one."

He folded his hands.

"Lieutenant," he said, "truth is not a single thing. It is a balance."

"A balance," I echoed.

"Yes. Between what happened and what can be allowed to matter."

I stepped closer to the desk and placed my palm flat on the folder.

"You think this ends with paper," I said. "You think if I sign this, the Ness forgets."

"The Ness," he said mildly, "is not our concern."

"No," I said. "That's your problem."

He rose then, slowly, as if sudden movement might invite resistance.

"You are being asked to perform a service," he said. "One final act of cooperation."

"And if I refuse?"

His gaze held mine.

"Then questions will be raised about your reliability. Your judgement. Your future usefulness."

There it was.

Not a threat.

A forecast.

"I've already been contained," I said. "You're just formalising it."

"You're dramatizing."

"I'm remembering."

He sighed.

"Lieutenant, Evelyn Selwyn was not cleared to be on that site. She had no official function. No documentation. She placed herself in danger."

"She was investigating her brother's disappearance."

"Which was not her remit."

"Neither was mine," I said. "But that didn't stop you calling me in."

He regarded me for a moment, reassessing.

"You are making this harder than it needs to be," he said.

"I imagine that's how Arthur Selwyn was described," I said. "Just before he became a problem."

The silence that followed was heavier now, no longer patient.

"Arthur Selwyn's death was an unfortunate industrial accident," he said.

"Was it?" I asked. "Because his body lay beneath an installation that officially doesn't exist."

He did not respond.

I took that as confirmation.

"You ordered it," I said. "Not you personally. But your office. Your chain."

"That is an allegation."

"It's an observation."

I returned to the chair and sat, deliberately, folding my hands in my lap.

"I will not sign this," I said.

The words felt solid when spoken, as though they had been waiting.

The man closed his eyes briefly.

"You understand the consequences?"

"I understand the cost," I said. "I watched it drown."

He opened his eyes again.

"You are refusing a direct instruction."

"Yes."

"On what grounds?"

"On the grounds that it is a lie."

He gathered the folder and tucked it under his arm.

"You will reconsider," he said.

"No," I replied. "I won't."

He paused at the door.

"You're choosing the wrong hill," he said. "This will not end the way you think."

I met his gaze.

"I don't think it ends at all," I said. "I think it leaks."

He left without another word.

I remained seated long after the door closed, listening to the wind worry the eaves, to the distant sound of men still clearing what remained of the wreckage. The Ness was quieter now, its violence spent, the storm having moved on to argue with some other coastline.

But quiet is not the same as empty.

I took the ledger from my coat and laid it on the desk.

It had been returned to me earlier that afternoon without comment, as though someone had decided it was no longer useful to confiscate it. That, too, was a calculation. Let the man keep his papers. Paper can be explained away. Paper can be burned.

Memory is less obliging.

I opened the ledger to the page I knew by heart.

Containment.

The word sat in the margin, steady and indifferent.

Evelyn's name appeared beneath it in Marwood's hand, neat, precise, already resigned to the outcome.

I closed the book again.

Outside, a lorry started up, its engine coughing before settling into a low, steady growl. More debris leaving the Ness. More silence was being transported inland.

They would write their report.

They would circulate it.

They would say the storm had erased the rest.

But my refusal was now part of the record too, whether they acknowledged it or not. An unsigned space has a presence all its own.

I stood and stepped outside.

The light was failing, the sky flattening into grey. The river moved through its new course without apology, stones clicking softly beneath its surface as it rearranged itself.

I walked to the place where Evelyn had died.

There was nothing to mark it.

No depression.

No stain.

Just water sliding past reeds that bent and rose again as if nothing had ever been disturbed.

"She died in the crash," they would say.

But the Ness does not lie.

It simply waits.

I turned back toward the huts, toward the men with their papers and their certainty.

They had asked me to sign away a woman's life.

I had refused.

That refusal would cost me.

I knew that as surely as I knew the tide would return.

But it would also cost them.

Because now, when the story was told, there would be a gap where my name should have been.

And gaps invite questions.

I put my hands in my pockets and began to walk.

The war would continue.

The War Office would survive.

But the truth, once denied a signature, has a way of finding other hands.

29

The envelope arrived in the afternoon, carried not by a runner or a clerk but by a man who had learned the value of being forgettable.

He did not ask my name. He did not announce himself. He waited just long enough for the door to open, placed the envelope on the small table by the wall, and stepped back as though the exchange had already been completed in his mind.

"From London," he said, and nothing more.

The paper was heavy. Cream, thick enough to resist folding, the flap sealed with red wax impressed by a device that suggested authority rather than beauty. There was no return address. There never is when the sender expects to be obeyed.

When the man had gone—and I watched him go, noting the way he walked as though the ground itself might be listening—I did not open it at once.

I had learned better.

I set the envelope down and made tea instead. The kettle took its time coming to a boil. The flame beneath it hissed softly, impatient, a sound I had come to associate with men who believed heat alone was a solution.

Outside, the Ness had returned to something like calm. The river slid through its new course without apology. The airfield beyond it lay altered but recognisable, a wounded thing already being translated into language that would make it survivable on paper.

The war had moved on.

That was the danger.

I poured the tea, let it steep, then carried the cup back to the table and sat opposite the envelope as though it were another person who might speak if allowed the space.

When I broke the seal, I did so carefully, peeling the wax back rather than tearing it. Old habits die slowly.

Inside were three things.

They were arranged deliberately, stacked in a way that suggested sequence rather than importance.

The first was a commendation.

The paper was lighter than the envelope but no less formal, headed with an insignia that required no explanation. The language was generous. Laudatory, even. It spoke of initiative under pressure, of service rendered beyond expectation, of composure in extraordinary circumstances.

It did not mention Evelyn Selwyn.

It did not mention Arthur.

It did not mention the river wall, or the underground chamber, or the list marked *Containment*.

It spoke instead of storms and damage and duty fulfilled.

I read it once, then again, and felt nothing at all.

Praise is easy when it costs nothing.

The second document was thinner.

A single page. No insignia this time. No letterhead. Just text, typed cleanly, the margins narrow enough to suggest urgency while pretending to restraint.

This was the warning.

It was phrased as concern.

It spoke of the toll of prolonged stress. Of the dangers of over-identification with an investigation. Of the importance of clarity and restraint when operating within sensitive theatres.

It suggested—without stating outright—that my judgement had been affected by recent events.

It did not accuse.

It implied.

That, too, is an art.

The third item was not folded at all.

A small card, heavier than it needed to be, slipped between the two papers like a blade between ribs.

No salutation.

No signature.

Just one sentence, typed in a hand that had never known doubt.

The matter is closed.

I placed the card back on the table and stared at it for a long time.

Closed.

It is an interesting word.

It suggests resolution without accounting. It implies that what lies behind it no longer requires attention, that whatever remains is either settled or irrelevant.

Closed doors are meant to be respected.

Closed files are meant to be forgotten.

Closed matters invite silence.

I folded the commendation first.

Carefully. Once. Then again. I placed it back into the envelope where it would not need to be seen again.

The warning followed. I read it once more, noting the phrasing, the careful absence of any specific allegation. It was a net rather than a blade. Useful if needed. Otherwise, content to wait.

I set that aside.

The card I left where it was.

Outside, a lorry passed along the inland track, its engine labouring briefly before settling into a steady growl. More debris leaving the Ness. More absence being managed.

I thought of Marwood then—not as she had been in the end, clinging to a failing wall, but as she had been before that: precise, calm, convinced. A woman who believed that order could be imposed long enough to matter.

"You still don't know who gave the order."

The river had taken her before she could say more.

And London had filled the silence.

I stood and crossed to the window.

From here, the river was only just visible, a dull ribbon catching the last of the light. The water had already learned its new path. It would not be persuaded back.

I wondered how many men would stand on its banks in years to come, pointing at it, explaining its course as though it had always been that way.

The commendation made a quiet sound as the envelope shifted on the table.

It was tempting, I thought, to accept it.

To take the paper, sign where required, return to London with a clean record and a heavier reputation. To let the matter be closed, as instructed.

Tempting—but not persuasive.

I returned to the table and picked up the card again.

The sentence had no punctuation beyond the full stop.

No room for discussion.

No acknowledgement of refusal.

It did not say *we believe* or *we conclude*.

It said *is*.

That was the difference.

I turned the card over.

Blank.

Of course.

I thought of Arthur Selwyn, tracing forbidden lines on a wet photographic plate, believing that once something was seen it must matter.

I thought of Evelyn, walking the Ness with silk hidden beneath wool, calm because she had already decided what she was willing to lose.

I thought of Liang Wei, setting stones into a wall he knew would fail, because someone had to stand there long enough for the water to be revealed.

And I thought of myself, sitting in a hut with a commendation I had not earned and a warning I did not accept, being told—politely, efficiently—to forget.

The kettle hissed again, though I had not put it back on the flame.

It was cooling.

Like the anger I had expected to feel and did not.

Anger burns out.

Resolve settles.

I took a pencil from my pocket.

Not a pen.

A pencil.

Ink suggests permanence. Pencil allows correction.

On the back of the commendation, in the wide margin beneath the formal language, I wrote a single line.

Refused.

I did not sign my name.

It did not need it.

I slid the commendation back into the envelope, the warning on top of it, the card last, so that it would be the first thing seen when the seal was broken again.

Then I closed the envelope and pressed the flap down without resealing it.

If they wanted it returned closed, they could do that themselves.

I left the envelope on the table and stepped outside.

The air smelled clean in the way it does after violence—washed, stripped of pretence. The sky was low but undecided, a pale sheet that might lift or might not.

Men were still working near the airfield, their movements smaller now, less urgent. The work of erasure had entered its careful phase.

I walked toward the river.

At the place where Marwood had fallen, there was still nothing to see. No marker. No disruption. Just water passing reeds that bent and rose again as though they had never known weight.

Closed, they would say.

But the river did not agree.

I crouched and dipped my fingers into the water, letting the cold settle into the skin. It moved around me without hesitation, carrying silt and fragments and things I could not name.

"You don't close a matter like this," I said aloud, though there was no one to hear me.

The water did not answer.

It did not need to.

When I returned to the hut, the envelope was still where I had left it.

I picked it up and carried it to the door.

The man who had delivered it was gone, of course. He would not return. Not yet.

I placed the envelope on the shelf beside the door, where it would be seen by anyone who entered.

Visible.

Unresolved.

That was the point.

I sat down and took out the ledger.

It felt heavier than before, though I knew its weight had not changed. I opened it to the page marked *Containment* and ran my finger down the names, stopping at Evelyn's.

Marwood had believed that lists could end things.

London believed that statements could.

I knew better now.

The matter was not closed.

It was merely unattended.

And unattended things, like rivers, have a way of finding their own course.

I closed the book and slid it back into my coat.

Outside, the light was fading again.

Another day ending without permission.

I poured out the tea, cold now, and rinsed the cup.

When the knock came later—softer this time, more tentative—I did not answer at once.

Let them wait, I thought.

Waiting teaches patience.

30

They moved him at dawn.

Not ceremonially. Not in secrecy either. Just efficiently, the way men move cargo they no longer wish to look at too closely. By the time I reached the outer fence, the lorry was already idling, breath steaming in the cold air, its canvas sides buttoned tight as if to prevent anything inconvenient from escaping.

Keller stood beside it under guard.

His hands were bound, but loosely now, more out of habit than necessity. He looked thinner than when I had first met him, his greatcoat hanging from his shoulders as if it belonged to someone else. The colour had gone from his face, replaced by a grey that spoke not of fear but of exhaustion—the kind that comes from having told the truth too often to people who do not wish to hear it.

A corporal checked a list. Another tightened a strap. No one spoke to Keller directly.

That mattered.

Men talk to prisoners when they are unsure what they have. They ignore them when the decision has already been made.

I stepped forward.

One of the guards shifted immediately, his hand moving toward his rifle with the reflexive irritation of a man who had already been told this was not my concern.

"Lieutenant," he said. "You're not authorised—"

"I'm aware," I replied. "So are you."

That gave him pause. Authority is a fragile thing. It depends entirely on who believes in it at the moment it is invoked.

I looked past him, at the lorry, at Keller.

"Where is he being sent?" I asked.

The corporal hesitated, then consulted his paper as if the answer might have changed.

"Another camp," he said. "Inland."

"Which one?"

"That information isn't for circulation."

I nodded. "Then it's accurate."

He did not like that, but he did not contradict it either.

Keller watched the exchange without expression. When our eyes met, he inclined his head slightly, the smallest acknowledgement. He had learned, I thought, how little movement was required to say what mattered.

I turned back to the corporal.

"Who ordered the transfer?" I asked.

"From London," he replied, too quickly.

"Of course," I said. "Did they tell you why?"

He swallowed. "Security considerations."

"Yes," I said. "They always do."

The lorry's engine coughed, then settled into a steady rhythm, the sound of a decision that would not be revisited.

The driver did not look down from his seat. He had been instructed not to.

I stepped closer to Keller, lowering my voice.

"They're blaming you," I said.

He nodded once. "I expected that."

"For what?"

"For surviving," he said simply.

I let that stand.

"You'll be questioned," I said. "Again. And again. They'll want you to change your account."

"I will not," he replied.

"They'll try to make it easier if you do."

He almost smiled. "They already tried to make it easier if I stopped talking."

That was Keller's strength, I had learned. He did not dramatise. He did not plead. He stated.

I glanced back toward the camp. From here, the airfield looked deceptively calm. Men moved between sheds. A crane lifted something long and twisted—part of the Zeppelin's frame, perhaps—and set it down where it would be cut into smaller, less recognisable pieces.

Erasure in progress.

I turned back to the guards.

"I want to speak to whoever authorised this," I said.

The corporal hesitated, then nodded toward the main huts. "You can try."

That, too, mattered.

I left Keller standing beside the lorry and walked back toward the administrative buildings, my boots sinking slightly into ground that had not yet decided what shape it preferred.

The river murmured somewhere behind me, moving through its new course with the quiet confidence of something that had already won the argument.

They were waiting for me.

Not in the hut I had been using, but in the larger office near the centre of the camp—the one with the reinforced walls, the stove that never quite warmed the room, and the desk positioned so that whoever sat behind it could look down on the space without appearing to do so.

Three men.

One in uniform. Two in civilian coats.

London does not travel alone.

The man in uniform did not rise when I entered.

"Lieutenant Quirk," he said. "You're becoming a habit."

"I've always had that effect," I replied.

One of the civilians—a tall man with narrow eyes and a voice that sounded as though it had been trained to carry no emotion—gestured to the chair opposite the desk.

"Sit," he said.

I did.

"You've been informed," he went on, "that the German airman is being transferred."

"Yes."

"This is a routine matter."

"No," I said. "It's a correction."

The second civilian—a broader man with a mouth that seemed permanently set in apology—cleared his throat.

"The prisoner's continued presence here poses a distraction," he said. "For morale."

"For whom?" I asked.

"For everyone," the uniformed officer replied. "Including you."

I leaned back slightly.

"You're removing a witness," I said.

The tall civilian smiled faintly. "Witnesses are unreliable."

"Not when they tell the truth," I said.

"Truth," he replied, "is not the issue."

"No," I agreed. "Control is."

The uniformed officer's jaw tightened.

"You're exceeding your remit again," he said.

"I don't have one," I replied. "You made sure of that."

That landed.

The broader civilian glanced at the tall one, then back at me.

"The German's account has been assessed," he said. "It contains inconsistencies."

"It contains inconvenience," I said.

"He's under stress," the uniformed officer added. "Disoriented. Guilt-ridden."

"Because he survived," I said.

"Because he is the enemy," the officer snapped.

"That makes him useful," I replied. "You don't need him to be believed. You just need him to be blamed."

Silence followed.

The tall civilian broke it.

"Lieutenant," he said, "this matter has already been resolved at a level above your concern."

"Yes," I said. "That's the problem."

He studied me for a moment, then folded his hands.

"You've shown persistence," he said. "That can be admirable. It can also be destructive."

"To whom?" I asked.

"To systems," he said.

"Good," I replied.

The broader civilian exhaled slowly.

"You're angry," he said.

"No," I said. "I'm attentive."

The uniformed officer stood.

"That's enough," he said. "The transfer will proceed."

"And Keller?" I asked. "What happens to him?"

The officer hesitated.

"He'll be interrogated further," he said. "Then reassigned."

"Or confined," I said.

"Or forgotten," the tall civilian added, not unkindly.

I rose.

"You're making a mistake," I said.

They did not react.

"You made it already," the uniformed officer replied.

I turned and left without another word. There was nothing else to be said in that room. Language had done all the damage it could.

Outside, the lorry was still idling.

Keller stood where I had left him.

I approached slowly, conscious of the guards watching, weighing whether to intervene. They did not. At this stage, there was little to gain by preventing conversation. The decision had already been made.

"They're taking you inland," I said.

"Yes."

"They'll ask the same questions."

"Yes."

"They'll want a different answer."

"Yes."

"And you won't give it."

"No."

I nodded.

"I can't stop this," I said.

"I know," Keller replied.

For a moment, neither of us spoke. The wind moved across the Ness, lifting grit and salt and the faint smell of oil from the cleared wreckage.

Then Keller surprised me.

"Thank you," he said.

"For what?" I asked.

"For believing me," he said.

The words were simple. Unadorned. They carried more weight than any commendation I had been offered.

"You told the truth," I said. "That was the simple part."

He shook his head slightly.

"No," he said. "Surviving was the straightforward part. Being believed was not."

One of the guards shifted, uncomfortable now.

"Time," he said.

Keller stepped toward the lorry, then stopped and turned back to me.

"They will say I imagined it," he said. "That the crash confused me. That guilt made me see things."

"Yes," I said.

"And they will say you encouraged this," he went on. "That you are unstable."

"Yes."

"And that what happened to the woman was an accident."

"Yes."

He held my gaze.

"But you know it was not," he said.

"Yes," I replied.

"That is enough," Keller said.

The guard opened the back of the lorry. Keller climbed in without resistance, turning once more before the canvas was pulled closed.

"I saw her argue," he said quietly. "She was not afraid. She was certain."

"I know," I said.

"And the man she argued with—"

"I know," I interrupted.

He nodded.

"Then remember," he said. "When they say there was no choice."

The canvas came down.

The latch was secured.

The engine revved, then the lorry pulled away, its tyres cutting fresh tracks into ground that would not remember them for long.

I stood there until it disappeared beyond the inland rise.

The Ness does not echo.

It absorbs.

I turned back toward the camp.

The War Office men were already leaving their hut, coats buttoned, expressions arranged into something approaching satisfaction. They did not look at me as they passed.

That, too, mattered.

The uniformed officer lingered.

"You did what you could," he said, almost kindly.

"No," I replied. "I did what I was allowed."

He frowned. "There's a difference?"

"Yes," I said. "One is permission. The other is responsibility."

He shook his head.

"You'll learn," he said.

"I already have," I replied.

He left without responding.

By evening, the Zeppelin's remains were gone entirely. Where it had fallen was now just another stretch of shingle and marsh, the land smoothing itself as though the interruption had never occurred.

I walked the perimeter alone.

At the place where Keller had first told me what he saw, there was nothing to mark it. At the place where Evelyn had been found, there was nothing. At the place where Marwood had fallen, the river ran as though it had always run that way.

The Ness remembers.

But it does not testify.

That part, I knew now, belonged to those who refused to forget.

I stopped at the edge of the river and watched the water move, carrying silt and fragments and the consequences of decisions made far from here.

Keller was gone.

Evelyn was gone.

Marwood was gone.

But the truth had not been transferred, or buried, or closed.

It had simply changed hands.

And this time, it had found someone willing to carry it without permission.

I turned back toward the huts as the light failed, the ledger heavy in my coat, the echo of Keller's words travelling with me.

Thank you for believing me.

It was the only commendation that mattered.

31

I did not decide all at once.

That is the lie men tell themselves later—that there was a moment, a line crossed, a word spoken that changed everything. In truth, the decision arrived the way water does on the Ness: by accumulation. A dampness you ignore at first. Then the slow realisation that your boots are already wet and the ground beneath them has no interest in your intentions.

The lorry carrying Keller was long gone by the time I returned to the hut.

The air inside smelled faintly of cold tea and damp paper. Someone had been in while I was away—not to search, not to steal, but to remind me of presence. A chair had been moved a fraction. A ledger not quite where I had left it. Small things. Corrections.

Containment does not announce itself. It edits.

I sat at the desk and opened the ledger again, though I knew every page by heart now. The names did not change when looked at a second time. They did not soften. If anything, they pressed back harder, ink asserting itself against the thinness of paper.

Arthur Selwyn.

Evelyn Selwyn.

Others, reduced to initials, then to numbers, then to nothing at all.

The War Office had told me the matter was closed.

They had been very clear about that.

Which meant, of course, that it was not.

I closed the book and rested my hands on the cover. They were steady. That surprised me. I had expected anger, or fear, or at least the tremor of something unspent. Instead, there was only a settled heaviness, the kind that comes when a choice has already been made somewhere below the level of language.

They would not stop.

Not with Keller removed.

Not with Marwood gone.

Not with a report unsigned and a commendation refused.

Containment does not end when it succeeds. It ends when it no longer needs to try.

I stood and stepped outside.

The Ness lay open under a low, undecided sky. The storm had scrubbed it clean, flattening the grasses, smoothing the shingle, redistributing the land with muted authority. The river ran through its alternative course as though it had always been meant to. Already, the place was becoming a story that could be told without difficulty.

That was the danger.

A figure stood near the walls remains, just inland of the bend where the stones had finally given way. He did not move when I approached, though I knew he had seen me long before I was close enough to speak.

Liang Wei.

He was not working now. His hands were clean. His coat buttoned against the cold. He stood with his weight balanced evenly, as though the ground beneath him was something to be listened to rather than used.

"They are finished for today," he said, without turning.

"Yes," I replied. "They always are."

We stood in silence for a while, watching the river slide past the broken stones. It no longer tested the wall. There was nothing left to argue with.

"They will say the storm did this," Liang said.

"They'll be right," I replied. "Just not in the way they mean."

He nodded once.

"The land is unsympathetic who is blamed," he said. "Only that weight is returned."

I glanced at him.

"You knew this would fail," I said.

"Yes."

"And you built it, anyway."

"Yes."

"Why?"

Liang turned then, meeting my gaze.

"Because sometimes," he said, "failure is the only way to show what was never meant to hold."

That, I realised, was the difference between us.

I had been trained to observe.

He had been trained to endure.

"They've taken Keller," I said.

"I saw."

"They'll blame him."

"Yes."

"They'll try to make him disappear."

Liang considered that.

"Some disappear loudly," he said. "Some quietly. The quiet ones last longer."

I thought of Keller's eyes as the lorry pulled away—not frightened, not pleading, only resolved in the way of a man who had already accepted what he could not control.

"He thanked me," I said.

Liang did not look surprised.

"For believing him," I went on.

"Yes," Liang said. "That matters."

"Does it?" I asked. "They're still taking him away."

Liang picked up a stone from the ground and rolled it between his fingers.

"When the river changes course," he said, "it does not ask whether the banks agree. It remembers where it was blocked."

He let the stone drop back into the water. It vanished without a sound.

"You cannot save everyone," he continued. "But you can decide what survives."

That was the decision, then.

Not whether to fight the War Office.

Not whether to confront London again.

But whether to allow the truth to remain where it could be shaped, softened, and ultimately erased?

I looked back toward the camp. Men moved between huts, their figures already smaller, already less urgent. The work of removal was nearly complete. By morning, there would be little left to suggest anything unusual had ever happened here.

Except memory.

Except paper.

Except the people who refused to look away.

"I'm going to expose it," I said.

Liang did not react.

"They'll call me disloyal," I went on. "Unstable. They'll say I interfered. That I imagined patterns. That grief made me reckless."

"Yes."

"They'll try to ruin me."

"Yes."

"They may succeed."

Liang nodded once.

"But they will not be able to say they were not told," he said.

I exhaled slowly.

"I don't know where to begin," I admitted. "Every channel leads back to them. Every desk answers to the same hand."

Liang reached into the inner pocket of his coat.

His actions were slow and intentional, as if he was reclaiming something he had resolved to part with long before.

He placed the object in my palm.

A pocket watch.

Silver scuffed at the edges, the casing dented where it had struck stone. The glass was cracked but intact. It was heavier than it looked, the weight of it settling immediately into my hand.

I did not need to open it to know what it was.

"Sgt. A. Pike," I said.

"Yes."

"You kept this."

"Yes."

"You knew what it meant."

"Yes."

I opened the watch anyway.

The hands were stopped at twenty-three minutes past five.

The time the argument by the river had ended.

The time Evelyn Selwyn had fallen.

"I found it the morning after," Liang said. "Here."

He gestured toward the bend, toward the place the river had already reclaimed.

"They told us not to speak of what we saw," he continued. "They told us the woman died in the crash."

"And you didn't believe them."

"No."

"Why not?"

Liang's mouth tightened slightly.

"Because lies are always hurried," he said. "And the truth had taken its time."

I closed the watch and held it for a moment longer than necessary.

"Why give this to me now?" I asked.

"Because you are leaving," Liang said.

"I haven't said that."

"You have," he replied. "With your body, if not your mouth. Men who intend to stay adapt. You are preparing to move."

He was right.

"You know this will make you visible," I said. "If they learn, you gave me this—"

"They already know I know something," Liang said. "That is enough."

He met my gaze, steady and unflinching.

"Some things must be remembered," he said.

The words did not sound like a warning.

They sounded like an instruction.

I closed my fingers around the watch.

It was no longer evidence alone. It was weight. A thing that had survived denial, water, and time.

"I don't know if it will be enough," I said.

Liang shrugged.

"Walls are never enough," he said. "But water remembers where they stood."

We walked together along the river for a short while, neither of us speaking. The land felt different now—not hostile, not welcoming, simply present in a way that could not be negotiated with.

At the edge of the camp, Liang stopped.

"This is where I return," he said.

"And me?"

"You go where words still travel," he said. "Before they are corrected."

I hesitated.

"They'll come after you," I said.

"They already have," he replied. "They simply haven't decided how."

That was the most honest thing he could have said.

We parted without ceremony.

I returned to the hut as the light thinned. Inside, the envelope from London still sat on the shelf by the door, unresolved and visible. I ignored it.

Instead, I laid the pocket watch beside the ledger on the desk.

Two objects.

Two truths.

One bureaucratic.

One human.

Together, they told a story that could not be reduced to weather or accident.

I made copies.

Not carefully.

Not perfectly.

Enough.

Names written out in full.

Dates noted.

Descriptions stripped of interpretation.

I did not write what I believed.

I wrote what I'd seen.

What I had been told.

What had been removed?

Keller's account.

Liang's watch.

The list marked *Containment*.

The refusal to sign.

Truth survives best when it is unadorned.

By the time night settled fully over the Ness, I had divided the material into packets small enough to carry, to hide, to lose without losing everything.

One would go to a journalist whose reputation for stubbornness exceeded his sense of safety.

One to a neutral intermediary who asked questions no government enjoyed answering.

One would not be sent at all, but kept, waiting for the moment denial became untenable.

I put the watch in my pocket.

It rested there with muted insistence, a reminder that time does not stop simply because someone wishes it to.

Outside, the river continued its work, unobserved and unpersuaded.

The War Office would say the matter was closed.

But memory had other plans.

32

I sent the packets before dawn because daylight invites second thoughts.

I did not linger over the act. Lingering gives weight to the wrong things. I walked, posted, walked again. Different routes. Different counters. Different hands receiving what they did not yet understand they were holding. By the time the sun thinned the cloud, the truth was no longer whole. It had been divided, and division was its protection.

The first packet held only names. Nothing else. No commentary, no accusation—just ink laid down plainly enough that no one could pretend confusion. It went to a man known for refusing to be hurried. I trusted that instinct more than ideology.

The second person brought along documents that were not intended to be sent elsewhere—notes, transfer forms, an unsigned report, and my written refusal where approval had been expected. It went somewhere neutral, to people who asked questions slowly and distrusted reassurance by default.

The third packet stayed with me.

The pocket watch rested inside my coat, heavy and cold, its stopped hands pressing against my ribs as if insisting on time's relevance. Sgt. A. Pike. Twenty-three minutes past five. The moment argument turned into consequence. That truth would move only when words proved insufficient.

By the time I turned back toward Orford Ness, there was no retrieving what I had done. That knowledge did not bring relief. It brought clarity.

The camp had settled into its careful quiet. Too careful. The Zeppelin was gone—cut down, carried off, translated into salvage and lists. The ground where it had fallen looked ordinary again, and that ordinariness was the most dangerous thing of all. Ordinary invites forgetting.

I walked past the huts without challenge. The men who mattered had already left. What remained was administration—habit in uniform. They were no longer looking for disruption, only completion. There was no need to offer them, either.

Out on the shingle, the Ness opened wide. No shelter. No ornament. Just land and water continuing their long argument without reference to human intent. The river ran through its alternative course as though it had always been meant to, stones clicking softly beneath the surface.

I stopped where wet sand met shingle and let the wind work at me.

Only then did the conflict arrive.

Not fear.

Not doubt.

Responsibility.

I had done what could not be undone. And now the question that followed was unavoidable: what would it cost to live with it?

This was not a local crime. It never had been. Orford Ness was a node, not an origin. The pattern extended outward once you allowed yourself to see it—cameras that saw too much, installations that did not exist, lists that decided who could remain. Containment was not a reaction to failure. It was a system designed to prevent inconvenience.

And systems do not end because one-man objects.

I felt the watch again, its weight a reminder that obedience had not saved Pike, and silence had not saved Evelyn, and the procedure had not saved Arthur Selwyn. I had not been trained for exposure. I had been trained to observe, to report, to withdraw when instructed.

This—what I was doing now—sat uneasily against that training.

London would not thank me. That much was certain. They would question my judgement, my stability, my usefulness. They would say I had over-identified that fatigue had narrowed my vision. They would offer me another assignment—quiet, distant, framed as trust restored.

And that was the conflict.

Because part of me wanted that.

Wanted the familiar shape of orders and purpose. Wanted the relief of believing that truth could be filed and left behind. Wanted to step back into the role that required observation but not consequence.

The other part of me knew that once a thing is seen clearly, it cannot be unseen.

The truth I had sent away would move without me now. Slowly. Inconveniently. It would surface in places that did not coordinate their denials. And when it did, the response would not be to correct the system, but to isolate the man who had made it visible.

That man was me.

I walked farther out until the sound of the sea erased everything else. The shingle shifted under my boots, each step provisional, each stone ready to give way if pressed too hard. I stopped where Evelyn Selwyn had once walked.

There was nothing to mark it.

No stain.

No depression.

No sign a stranger could recognise.

The Ness had already taken what it would.

I knelt and let the shingle slide through my fingers. Each stone had been broken, carried, returned. None of them remembered the shape they began with. That was how the truth would travel now—not intact, not clean, but persistent.

Somewhere inland, Keller was being questioned again, his words already translated into doubt. Somewhere else, files were being closed, stamped, archived. Somewhere higher still, men were deciding how to manage what could not yet be dismissed.

They did not know what I had done.

That was intentional.

Exposure is not an explosion.

It is a seep.

I stood and looked out to sea, thinking of the next assignment already waiting—another place, another name, another set of instructions delivered as though the last had never existed. I could accept it. I could go. I could perform competence and call it duty.

Or I could carry this forward.

Not a confession.

Not a crusade.

But as a refusal.

The wind rose, lifting grit and salt, flattening the horizon. For a moment the Ness looked as it must have long before men-built walls and secrets upon it—empty, indifferent, unclaimed.

It was none of those things.

It held the memory.

It always had.

I lowered my head and spoke, not for effect, not to be heard, but because some words belong to the land that taught them.

"The Ness remembers."

The wind took the words and carried them out over the water.

I turned back across the shingle then, leaving no footprints that would last, carrying with me what could not be erased. The truth was no longer contained.

THE END

Don't miss out!

Visit the website below and you can sign up to receive emails whenever Andrew Hixson publishes a new book. There's no charge and no obligation.

https://books2read.com/r/B-A-IWTC-GSNBJ

BOOKS 2 READ

Connecting independent readers to independent writers.

Did you love *Murder on Orford Ness*? Then you should read *Murder on Mersea Island*[1] by Andrew Hixson!

[2]

"***Murder on Mersea Island***" by Andrew Hixson introduces recently retired military intelligence officer Silas Quirk as he investigates the mysterious locked-room death of his friend Sir Geoffrey Linton at a reclusive manor on Mersea Island, uncovering hidden passages, cryptic clues, and complex relationships among the household members, while contending with local inspector Alice Hargreaves and the housekeeper Winifred Hall's guarded legacy amidst a setting charged with secrecy and tension.

---

1. https://books2read.com/u/bwJjZP
2. https://books2read.com/u/bwJjZP

About the Author

Andrew Hixson was born in Barnet in 1958 and spent his formative years in North Finchley, where he attended school. After his education, Andrew embarked on a career working at the renowned Smithfield Meat Market in London. It was later in life, upon relocating to Suffolk, that he met his wife and settled into family life. Andrew is the proud father of two daughters and grandfather to three granddaughters, as well as two much-loved grand-dogs. Though Suffolk is now his home, he remains an ardent supporter of Arsenal Football Club. A keen reader, Andrew draws inspiration from the works of Tim Weaver, Richard Osman, and Agatha Christie, whose books are among his favourites.

www.ingramcontent.com/pod-product-compliance
Ingram Content Group UK Ltd.
Pitfield, Milton Keynes, MK11 3LW, UK
UKHW041829150326
468994UK00001B/372

9 798233 880230